CONSTITUTION

STAR TREK®

MY BROTHER'S KEEPER
BOOK TWO OF THREE

CONSTITUTION

MICHAEL
JAN
FRIEDMAN

POCKET BOOKS
New York London Toronto Sydney Tokyo Singapore

An *Original* Publication of POCKET BOOKS

POCKET BOOKS, a division of Simon & Schuster Inc.
1230 Avenue of the Americas, New York, NY 10020

STAR TREK is a Registered Trademark of
Paramount Pictures.

A VIACOM COMPANY

This book is published by Pocket Books, a division of
Simon & Schuster Inc., under exclusive license from
Paramount Pictures.

ISBN: 0-671-01919-8

First Pocket Books printing January 1999

10 9 8 7 6 5 4 3 2 1

POCKET and colophon are registered trademarks of
Simon & Schuster Inc.

Printed in the U.S.A.

For Joe Simko

CONSTITUTION

Chapter One

SECURITY OFFICER Scott Darnell would have preferred to go to the funeral. As it was, it had fallen to him to stand watch in the *Enterprise*'s monitor-studded security section, overlooking the ship's internal sensor net and guarding her phaser stores.

Hardly anyone ever visited security unless he himself was a security officer. So when the door slid aside to admit First Officer Spock, Darnell was a little surprised. Then he saw the phaser rifle cradled in the Vulcan's arms and he understood.

Spock had commandeered the rifle shortly after the *Enterprise* established orbit around Delta Vega. Darnell hadn't been on duty at the time, but the inventory file showed the incident clearly enough.

What it didn't show was why the first officer had needed the weapon. As far as Darnell or most anyone

1

else knew, they had only made a stop at Delta Vega to obtain the hardware they required to repair their warp drive. The planetoid being completely unoccupied, it didn't seem a phaser rifle would be of much utility to anyone there.

Nonetheless, Spock had taken the weapon and beamed down with it. And sometime after that, something terrible had happened on Delta Vega—something, it seemed, which wasn't entirely unexpected, or why bring down a rifle in the first place?

When it was over, three of the crew had died. One was Gary Mitchell, the primary navigator. The second was Elizabeth Dehner, a psychiatrist who had joined the *Enterprise* only recently. And the third was Lee Kelso, the man whose funeral Darnell was missing.

But that was all the security officer knew. In fact, that was all anyone knew. The captain had classified the matter, prohibiting all those who had beamed down to Delta Vega from speaking of it.

It didn't seem fair to Darnell—especially when people had lost their lives down there. But that was the way it was, and there was nothing he or any of his colleagues could do about it.

"Mr. Spock," he said as the Vulcan approached. "I guess you're returning that rifle now."

"Indeed," Spock replied, handing it over.

Darnell took a quick look at the weapon. It had a few dinks, but otherwise appeared to be in good condition. Then, just out of habit, he checked to see if there was any charge left.

He was confused. What's more, he said so.

"Why is that?" the Vulcan inquired, his lean visage characteristically devoid of emotion.

"Well," the security officer explained, "I figured with all that happened down there—whatever that might have been—someone would have had occasion to squeeze off a few shots."

Spock cocked an eyebrow. "There are two possibilities, Mr. Darnell. Either the rifle was fired and someone recharged it, perhaps to avoid any official record of its having been employed on Delta Vega . . . or contrary to your expectations, it never was fired. However, as the matter is now classified, I do not believe it is appropriate to speculate either way."

With that, the first officer turned and departed, leaving the security officer with the fully charged rifle in his hands. Darnell grunted. Then he got up from his seat among the security monitors and headed for the ordnance locker to put the rifle back where it belonged.

Vulcans, he thought. *Why can't they just say what they mean?*

Lieutenant Hikaru Sulu knelt in the *Enterprise*'s botany lab, a place of vibrant colors and exotic scents, and contemplated the Mandreggan moonblossoms he had been cultivating.

Their large, fragile-looking petals were a pale yellow at the center, fading to white and then deepening into a lush scarlet at the edges. They were breathtakingly beautiful. Even First Officer Spock had remarked on their appearance, and he seldom remarked on anything that didn't pertain to the ship's operation.

No one had believed that he could grow moonblossoms in an artificial environment. After all, no starship botanist had ever done it before. But he accomplished it anyway.

After all, Sulu was the kind of man who did what he set out to do. When he was a teenager, he had set his sights on attending Starfleet Academy and earned himself a place at that prestigious institution. And when he had made the decision to specialize in astrophysics, he landed a berth on one of the most prestigious vessels in the fleet.

In fact, in all his twenty-seven years, he had never failed to obtain something he really wanted. So why had it been so difficult for him to go after the thing he had come to desire lately?

Of course, the astrophysicist knew the answer to that question. After all, life was good on the *Enterprise*. He had comforts here he had grown used to, friends he wouldn't look forward to giving up.

But as Sulu's grandfather once told him, "Observe the wisdom of the shark, Hikaru. It knows that if it stops swimming, it stops breathing. So it continues to swim."

Like the shark they had seen at the aquarium that day, he would continue to swim. But that didn't make it any easier to abandon the life he had made for himself there.

"Hikaru?" came a voice.

Sulu looked up and saw two of his fellow crewmen standing at the entrance to the botany lab. One was Daniel Alden, the ship's primary communications officer. The other was Joe Tormolen, a lieutenant in engineering. It was Tormolen who had called his name.

"Come on," he said.

"It's time," Alden added.

Knowing seats would be at a premium at the funeral service, Sulu nodded and got to his feet. "Just saying goodbye to some of my friends," he explained as he joined the others.

"I know the feeling," said the communications officer.

Sulu smiled wistfully. "That's right. I guess you would."

Together, they left the botany lab and headed for the *Enterprise*'s chapel. And when they got there, Sulu thought, he would be saying goodbye to another friend. He would miss Lee Kelso, he reflected.

He would miss them all.

Captain James T. Kirk entered the *Enterprise*'s small, spartan chapel, with its silver-blue walls and its neatly arranged rows of chairs and its lonely, red-orange lectern. Looking around, he scanned the solemn faces of the crewmen who had already arrived for the noontime service.

There must have been a hundred of them, from every section of the ship and every deck, representing every rank and every species in the Fleet, all gathered to pay their respects to a man they had valued and loved and admired. And if there weren't enough chairs in the place for nearly a third of those in attendance, that didn't seem to daunt them any.

Kelso would have been touched by the size of the

turnout, Kirk thought. Touched and more than a little amazed.

In one corner of the room, Montgomery Scott, the chief engineer, was speaking wistfully with Lieutenant Tormolen and Ensign Beltre, no doubt recounting some fond remembrance of the dead man. In another corner, Yeoman Smith and Lieutenant Alden were commiserating over their loss with Lieutenant Sulu of astrophysics. And in still another corner, Chief Medical Officer Piper was exchanging stoic looks with Lieutenant Dezago and Nurse Chapel.

Several other crewmen had asked to attend also, but regulations required a full complement of specialists to operate the Constitution-class vessel. That was especially true on the bridge, where Ensign Green had taken over the helm controls, Lieutenant Brent had moved to navigation, Lieutenant Farrell was manning the communications console, and Lieutenant Commander Spock, the *Enterprise*'s Vulcan first officer, had assumed temporary command of the ship.

"Captain," said Scott, noticing Kirk's entrance. He approached his commanding officer. "We've been waitin' for ye, sir."

The captain nodded, adjusting the plastiform cast Piper had given him to help his wrist injury heal. "Sorry I'm late, Scotty. Something came up at the last minute."

The engineer looked at him suspiciously. "If I may ask, sir, what sort of something was it?"

Kirk smiled at him, knowing the pride the man took in his work. "Just a little trouble with the plasma manifold. But from what I'm told, it can wait until the service is over."

Scott's features puckered into a frown. "Are ye sure, sir? If ye like, I could take a moment t'—"

The captain held up his good hand to restrain the engineer. "Quite sure, Scotty. We've kept everyone waiting long enough."

Scott nodded dutifully. "As ye say, sir."

In the thirteen months since Kirk had taken command of the *Enterprise,* he had used the ship's chapel to hold five weddings, an Iltrasian coming-of-age ceremony, and only one funeral—that of a young lieutenant named Henry George Beason, who had been killed in the weapons room when it took a hit from an Orion mercenary.

Of course, Beason wasn't the only casualty of Kirk's stint as commanding officer, or even the first. However, the captain hadn't conducted services for the fourteen who had died previously. It was only customary to do so when a crewman lacked family and friends planetside.

Beason's only surviving relative had been a maiden aunt in Murfreesboro, Tennessee, who was too feeble to leave her house, much less attend any kind of funeral for her nephew. As a result, the captain had arranged a service for the man on the *Enterprise.*

Unfortunately, the situation was a similar one today. The deceased was an orphan, a man who had been raised in an institution outside Los Angeles. The only people he really cared about—and the only people who cared about him—were his fellow crewmen. It was only fitting that his death be marked by a service aboard the ship.

Finding a seat in the front row, Kirk found himself flanked by security officers Matthews and Rayburn on one hand and Lieutenant Stiles on the other. Stiles, a severe-looking man who had shown himself to be an efficient officer, turned to the captain.

"Sir," he said, acknowledging Kirk's presence.

"Stiles," Kirk said in return.

"Hell of a way to go," Stiles remarked. He shook his head. "Choked to death with a cable. Nasty business all around."

The captain was forced to agree. "It certainly was."

"There've been plenty of tragedies in my family," Stiles told him somberly. "We lost a half-dozen brave souls in the Romulan Wars alone. But choked to death with a cable . . ."

"Sir?" said Rayburn, who was seated closer to Kirk than Matthews was.

The captain turned to him, glad for the opportunity to speak to someone besides the morbid Stiles. "Yes, Lieutenant?"

"Is it true what they say about Lieutenant Mitchell and Dr. Dehner?" Rayburn asked. "That they died heroes as well?"

"I don't know what's being said," Kirk told him, adjusting his cast again, "and as you know, I'm not at liberty to discuss the details. However, my log reflects that Lieutenant Mitchell and Dr. Dehner died in the line of duty. That should tell you something."

Rayburn thought about it for a moment, then smiled. "Thank you, sir. I think I understand."

He didn't, of course. The security officer didn't have any inkling of the fate that had befallen Lieutenant Mitchell and Dr. Dehner. But then, that was the way the captain wanted it.

After all, neither Mitchell nor Dehner had asked to become something more than human. Neither of them had wanted to hurt their colleagues in any way. With that in mind, it wouldn't have been fair to label them monsters in the official record.

A moment later, Kirk's attention was drawn to the lectern, where Scotty was standing and making a point of clearing his throat. Kirk gave the engineer his attention. So did everyone else eventually, even the crewmen forced to stand in the back.

Scotty looked around. "Ye all know why we're gathered today, in such numbers it puts the size o' this wee, cramped chapel t' shame. We're here t' say goodbye and godspeed to our friend, Lee Kelso."

A murmur of agreement ran through the assemblage. After all, Kelso had been one of their favorites. He had enriched a lot of lives in his short time on the *Enterprise*.

The engineer gestured and a man-sized duranium container, supported by an antigravity cart, appeared in the chapel's doorway. The man and woman attending the container, both of them ensigns in the science section, guided it into the room and positioned it next to Scotty.

Taking a moment to consider it, the engineer smiled a wistful smile. "If Kelso were here with us now, I believe he'd be wonderin' what all the fuss was about. After all, he'd say, he was just doin' his duty—

9

what any one of us would've done under the same circumstances. As ye know, he wasn't one t' toot his own horn."

True enough, the captain thought. Kelso had been so self-effacing at times, Kirk had felt the urge to grab the helmsman and impose on him how important his contribution was.

At the lectern, the Scotsman shrugged. "I don't have to tell ye we were competitors, Kelso and I. Sure, he was a helmsman by trade, but the man prided himself on his engineerin' ability and his overall efficiency. And, as ye may have noticed, so do I."

The captain couldn't help but chuckle at the remark. He wasn't alone in that regard.

"The day I met him," Scotty continued, "Kelso had just come over from the *Potemkin.* I found the lad putterin' around on a catwalk in engineerin', his face screwed up tight in concentration, makin' wee adjustments to the deuterium injectors."

Kirk could picture Kelso doing something like that. There was another ripple of laughter from the audience.

"When I asked him what he was up to," said Scotty, "he told me he was tryin' t' get a bit more power out o' the engines. Apparently, some idiot of a chief engineer had everythin' set in the wrong ratios."

This time, the laughter was louder—loud enough to echo from the bulkheads. Scotty grinned and shook his head.

"As ye know," he said, "Kelso and I were often on landing party teams together. What ye may nae know is that we used t' race like wee lads t' see who could make it to the transporter pad first."

Really, Kirk thought. Had he been aware of something like that, he would have put a stop to it. Unfortunately, Kelso wouldn't be doing any more racing, so the issue had become academic.

"Of course," Scotty noted, "I had a decided advantage, considerin' the bridge is farther from the transporter room than engineerin' is. And anyway, I never had t' wait for a replacement before I could take off. All I ever had t' do was give a few orders and be on my way."

That must have frustrated Kelso no end, Kirk mused. The man hated to come in second in anything—even tic-tac-toe.

"Then," the engineer continued, "a few weeks ago, we ran into that Ceebriian derelict near Alpha Ortelina Seven, and the captain asked me and Kelso t' meet him in the transporter room." He shrugged. "Mind ye, havin' anticipated the summons, I was as ready as I'd ever been in my life. I left engineerin' at a brisk but confident pace, knowin' there was nae way Kelso could beat me to my destination.

"And yet," said Scotty, "when I reached the transporter room, there the lad was—grinnin' as if he'd swallowed th' galaxy's largest canary. And he was nae even breathin' heavy, a sure sign I'd been hoodwinked."

The engineer shook his head. "It was nae until the next day that I forced the truth out o' the rascal. With the help of a transporter operator who'll remain nameless for her own good, he had reprogrammed the bloody controls—fixin' it so a signal from the helm console would activate a special subroutine. A minute later, by which time Kelso would already have entered the turbolift, the transporter would activate itself—and he'd be beamed directly to the transporter platform."

Stiles shot a look at the captain. "Interesting."

Kirk was more than a little discomfited by the tale. "You can say that again," he replied.

"And now," said Scotty, "we'll hear from Lieutenant Dezago."

The lieutenant, a man with blunt features and closely cropped brown hair, was the ship's backup communications officer. Taking the engineer's place at the lectern, he scanned the faces in the audience.

"I wish I could tell you I shared a lot of funny moments with Lee Kelso," he began. "Maybe I did and I just don't remember them; I guess that would be my loss. What I do remember is this—lying beside a crashing waterfall on Arronus Seven, my forehead bleeding from a three-inch gash and my right leg broken in two places, while a half-dozen Klingons advanced through the jungle to finish me off."

The captain recalled the incident—a simple survey mission turned deadly. But then, how were they to know the planet's crust contained mineral desposits the Klingons coveted?

"I thought I was a dead man," said Dezago, "and they'd be shipping me back to Earth in a duranium container just like this one. Then, all of a sudden, I saw Kelso kneeling beside me. I don't think he'd mind my saying he looked scared. Petrified, in fact. After all, there were a lot more of those Klingons than there were of us, and the vast likelihood was that we would both die on that ball of mud fifty light-years from home."

The communications officer's brow furrowed as he remembered. "But I'm here to tell you Kelso stood his ground, scared or not. He stayed there with me, and he just kept firing and firing, and I kept firing too—and after what seemed like an impossibly long time, the captain and Mr. Spock arrived with a squad's worth of reinforcements."

The assemblage was quiet, but all eyes were on Dezago.

"I wish I had been there on Delta Vega when Kelso was killed," declared the communications officer. He bit his lip. "I wish . . . I had had a chance to do for Kelso what he did for me."

As the audience maintained its respectful silence, Dezago sat down and was patted on the back by his neighbors. A moment later, Scotty came to stand behind the lectern again.

"That was our Lieutenant Kelso," the engineer said. "Was it nae? The lad was always plungin' ahead, always hellishly determined t' do his duty, nae matter the difficulties involved or the danger."

His breath caught in his throat for just a second. Then he thrust out his chin and went on.

"I believe Ensign Beltre would like t' say a few words as well." Scotty turned to the woman. "Ensign?"

Beltre, a darkly attractive security officer with a

long, black ponytail and light green eyes, came around to the lectern. Scotty stood aside to make room for her.

"As most of you know," Beltre said a little tentatively, her eyes flicking from one face to the other, "I'm still pretty new on the ship. I didn't know Lieutenant Kelso as long or as well as some of you. Still, I knew him well enough to have some idea of how much we've lost.

"Not so long ago—a couple of weeks, I guess—I was sitting by myself in the rec lounge, having a cup of coffee and reading a monograph on phaser failures. I probably would've been happier sitting with other people," Beltre noted, "but I didn't really know anyone at the time, and I'm not the type to go around introducing myself.

"Then Lieutenant Kelso walked in. I didn't take any particular notice of him at the time. After all, he was a face like any other. But a moment later, I looked up and saw him standing there with a steaming cup of something hot in each hand.

"He didn't tell me his name. He didn't ask me mine. He just put one of the cups down in front of me, smiled and told me it was his special blend. Then he walked away and sat down elsewhere.

"Instantly, I saw the genius of what the man had done. He had invited me to join him if I liked, but he hadn't placed any obligation on me to do so. So if I really wanted to keep on reading that monograph, I could have done it without any problem. And on the other hand, if I really wanted company, I could have had that, too.

"Preferring the company to the monograph," said Beltre, "I picked up my new cup of coffee and joined him. We had a great conversation. In a matter of minutes, the lieutenant became one of my favorite people. After a while, I even became comfortable enough to tell him how clever he was to have offered me that cup."

She sighed. "He told me he had spent some time in an orphanage, and he had experienced enough loneliness there to last him a lifetime. When he got out, he said, he had promised himself he would never let anyone else feel lonely if he could help it, and he hadn't gone back on that promise yet."

The ensign looked around. "As I said before, I may not have known Lieutenant Kelso as well as some of you. But I can tell you this . . . no one's going to miss him more than I will."

And so it went.

One crewman after another stood up to pay tribute to Kelso, regaling the tightly packed assemblage with anecdote after anecdote, until almost everyone present had said a word or two. Kirk listened to description after description of the dead man's bravery, of his kindness, of his dedication and his antic sense of humor.

Then it was *his* turn.

"Sir?" said Scotty.

Kirk nodded and got up from his seat. Advancing to the lectern, he took hold of it in both hands—the injured one as well as the uninjured—and surveyed the faces of his audience. It was plain that his people were looking to him for solace and inspiration in their time of travail. After all, he was their commanding officer.

He hoped he wouldn't disappoint them.

"You've all done Lieutenant Kelso proud," the captain began, "with your stories about what he meant to you. Clearly, he touched each of us in a profound way, a way someone else might not have been aware of. I could tell you a couple of stories of my own, I suppose . . . about how I relied on Lee Kelso and was never disappointed by him, about how I came to admire his uncommon blend of gentleness and ferocious determination.

"But those tales have already been told, for the most part, and I could never match the eloquence and devotion with which you told them. So," he said, "let me tell you a different kind of story."

Scotty smiled a wistful smile. After all, he had organized this service and already had an idea of what Kirk was going to say.

"About a year and a half ago," the captain noted, "I was reviewing personnel records, putting together a crew for my first command as a starship captain. No easy task, I can tell you that. In any case, about halfway through the process, I came across an ensign named Lee Kelso who had applied for a transfer from the *Potemkin*.

"Looking over the man's file, I saw a number of items that interested me. He had posted excellent grades at the Academy. His service record on the *Lexington* and then on the *Potemkin* was spotless, and he was acknowledged as one of the most proficient helmsmen in the Fleet."

There were murmurs of agreement from several crewmen in the audience. After all, they knew the truth of the matter. They had seen the lieutenant's work at the helm for themselves.

"But according to a notation at the bottom of the screen," Kirk went on, "Lee Kelso didn't have much of a future as an officer in Starfleet. No future? I repeated to myself. I wondered about that. It didn't seem to make any sense in light of all his credentials. Unfortunately, his file didn't tell me why that notation had been made.

"Curious, I contacted Kelso's captain on the *Potemkin,* whose acquaintance I'd made at a Starfleet cocktail party a couple of years earlier. After exchanging a few pleasantries, I asked him why he had cast doubt on Kelso's potential as an officer.

"I remember the captain sighing, smiling sympathetically, and saying five short words: *He cares too damned much.* I asked him to elaborate. The captain was kind enough to comply.

"'Kelso's neurotic, Jim,' he told me. 'He feels compelled to go over and over every last detail of his work until he feels he's gotten it perfect. Someday, he's just going to explode.'

"I thanked the captain for his time," Kirk said, "and signed off. Then, as fast as I possibly could, I contacted Starfleet Command and put in a request. I told them I didn't care who else they gave me—at all costs, I wanted a man named Lee Kelso."

A few heads bobbed approvingly, telling him that was the Kelso they had known, too. Then someone in the audience started clapping, and someone

17

else joined him, and before long the entire chapel was resounding with approval for Kirk's words.

No, thought the captain—not the words. What they're clapping for is who the words were about. Kelso meant that much to them.

The applause went on for a long time—more than a minute, Kirk estimated. As it began to die down, the captain walked over to the intercom panel in the wall behind him.

"Kirk to transporter room," he said.

"Kyle here, sir," came the response.

"Ready?" asked the captain.

"Ready," the transporter operator assured him.

Kirk considered the metal container that held his helmsman's body. Then he spoke again, his voice thick with emotion. "I commend the mortal remains of Lee Kelso to the stars he loved so dearly. May he always rest peacefully in their midst."

Everyone in the chapel joined him in the sentiment, bidding their colleague farewell in their own words.

"Bye, Lee," one declared.

"We'll miss you," another promised.

"Good voyage," said a third.

The captain tried to ignore the tightening in his throat. "Energize, Mr. Kyle."

The air around Kelso's coffin began to shimmer with iridescent light. Slowly, gradually, the duranium container began to fade from view. Then both the light and the coffin were gone.

A thousand meters from the ship, Kirk told himself, there was something new floating in the endless void of space, glinting in the light of distant stars. In life,

Lee Kelso hadn't asked for any special honors, nor would he have asked for any in death. Nonetheless, the captain was pleased that the man had at last gotten the recognition he deserved.

Kirk remembered the others who had perished on Delta Vega and felt the weight of regret. His friend Gary would never have his remains beamed into space. Neither would Elizabeth Dehner, who had given her young life to save his. Both of them had been buried on the planetoid—Gary in a grave of his own making, Dehner in one the captain had hollowed out of the rock with the last of his phaser charge.

Certainly, Kirk would have liked to bring their bodies back to Earth, where both of them had spent their childhoods. Their loved ones deserved that much, at least.

But considering what Gary and Dehner had become, considering the incredibly dangerous power they had wielded, the captain couldn't take the chance that there might be some spark of life left in them—a spark, perhaps, that Federation technology wasn't sophisticated enough to detect.

So he had left them there in the wilderness near the dilithium-cracking plant, in a place which would soon be designated off-limits to anyone but the most highly trained security teams. He had abandoned his best friend and the woman who had saved the universe from a burgeoning god, and in doing so had left behind a piece of his soul as well.

As the chapel began to fill with the piped-in strains of "Amazing Grace," Kirk saw a tear collect in the corner of Scotty's eye. He put his good hand on the engineer's shoulder and squeezed it.

Scotty looked at him and managed a sad, wistful smile. He seemed to say, We sent the wee lad off right, did we nae, sir? And the captain couldn't help but agree.

Kelso's service was all but over, he reflected. But Gary Mitchell's still loomed ahead of him, back on Earth—and, for Kirk at least, Gary's would be the tougher one by far.

Chapter Two

As KIRK wound his way along the stark, metal corridor, headed for the *Enterprise*'s briefing room, he still felt the solemn atmosphere of Lee Kelso's funeral service hovering around him like a tenacious wisp of fog. He still heard the haunting cadences of "Amazing Grace" and saw the burden of sadness in the haggard faces of his crewmen.

Then the door to the briefing room slid aside and he saw Spock waiting for him within. His first officer was already seated at the long, oval table that dominated the compartment. Bent over a data padd that he held in his hand, Spock's features were thrown into relief by its faint, green glow.

The captain studied the severe lines of the Vulcan's profile, wondering which Spock he would find there—the one who had remained aloof from his comrades'

21

emotional exchanges for the first year of their mission together, or the one who had attempted to reach out to Kirk in his moment of grief over Gary Mitchell's death.

Slowly, the first officer turned from his data padd to face him. His dark eyes were alert, probing, his brow wrinkled ever so slightly.

"Captain," he said.

Kirk nodded. "Spock."

"I trust the funeral went well," the Vulcan speculated.

It wasn't so much what Spock said as the way he said it—a nuance of inflection, a subtle difference in his tone. The Vulcan wasn't just being polite, the captain noted. He seemed genuinely interested in what had transpired in the ship's chapel.

So it was *that* Spock, Kirk thought—the one who had expressed a desire to comfort him in his extremity. The captain was glad. After all, that was the Spock he had come to prefer.

"It went very well," Kirk replied. "I'd venture to say there wasn't a dry eye in the house."

The Vulcan's brow wrinkled. "A dry eye . . . ?" Then understanding dawned. "You're referring to the practice of shedding tears on behalf of the deceased. Another human custom."

The captain smiled a sad smile. "Not just a custom, Spock. We don't weep at will. It's a reflex."

The first officer absorbed the information as if it were the boiling point of molybdenum—that is, with great interest. "Intriguing," he said. And then he added, with just the vaguest hint of an apology, "As you know, Vulcans do not weep."

"I'm aware of that," Kirk assured him. "But don't worry, Commander. I won't hold it against you."

The Vulcan tilted his head quizzically and arched an eyebrow. "Was that an attempt at humor, sir?"

The captain sighed. "An attempt," he conceded. Then he noted the information displayed on the three-sided monitor in the center of the table. "Shall we get started?"

"By all means," said Spock.

Using his padd as a remote control, he brought up a list on the monitor. A personnel list, Kirk thought, with all proposed changes in the composition of the crew.

The first officer had scheduled this meeting a long time ago—well before they had probed the energy barrier at the galaxy's perimeter or seen the captain's friend turn into a superhuman terror. Spock had offered to postpone the session in light of all that had happened, but Kirk had insisted they go through with it.

There was still an *Enterprise,* after all, and it still carried upward of four hundred sentient beings through the vastness of space. They hadn't all perished on Delta Vega.

The captain took a seat on the opposite side of the table. "Fire away," he told the Vulcan.

Impassively, Spock turned to the monitor and read the first name on the list. "Lieutenant Daniel Alden."

"Alden," Kirk acknowledged.

"The lieutenant has requested a transfer to the Federation research colony on Delanos Six," said the first officer. "Apparently, his fiancée was appointed chief administrator of the colony two days ago, though Alden received the news only last night."

Kirk nodded approvingly. Alden had warned him that his fiancée was in line for such a post, though he wasn't in a position to predict when it might come through.

"Good for her," said the captain. Then he amended his remark. "Good for both of them."

He had met Alden's fiancée the last time the crew had taken shore leave on Earth. The woman was bright, capable . . . everything the Federation looked for in a colony administrator.

Beautiful, too. Alden was a lucky man.

"Transfer granted," Kirk noted. "I'll congratulate the lieutenant personally first chance I get. Who's next?"

Spock consulted his padd. "Yeoman Barbara Smith."

The captain grunted. "She's requested a transfer as well?"

"She has, sir."

"To what ship?" Kirk inquired.

"To any ship," the Vulcan replied.

The captain winced. He didn't suppose it helped that he had gotten the woman's name wrong on several occasions. As recently as the day they had tried to pierce the energy barrier at the limits of the galaxy, he had referred to her as "Jones."

But, of course, that wasn't the main reason Smith

was leaving. The yeoman simply hadn't been comfortable from the day she set foot on the *Enterprise*. Kirk couldn't begin to say why, nor could she or anyone else. It just worked out that way sometimes.

Being a trooper, Smith had stuck it out for nearly a year. There was no point in her sticking it out any longer.

"Transfer granted," said Kirk. "Let the rest of the Fleet know the yeoman is available . . . and that she's got my highest endorsement. That should help her out a bit."

"Aye, sir," Spock replied, making the appropriate entry on his data padd. "Shall I go on?"

"Please," the captain told him.

The first officer hesitated for a moment before reading the next name out loud. "Dr. Mark Piper," he said at last, "requests a discharge from active service, effective at your earliest convenience."

"Piper?" said Kirk.

The name caught the captain off guard—but only for a moment. After all, he reflected, his chief medical officer had been talking about retirement more and more lately.

And come to think of it, hadn't Piper mentioned a half-dozen standing invitations from children and grandchildren to come live with them? Maybe he had finally accepted one of them.

Well, Kirk told himself, if that was what the old boy wanted, more power to him. Piper had been a capable and compassionate physician for more than fifty years, his career stretching back even before the Federation's first contact with the Klingons. The man deserved to spend the rest of his life any damned way he wanted.

The only problem was replacing him. There just weren't that many Mark Pipers in the universe. Having gotten lucky once, Kirk didn't have much faith in it happening again.

With mixed feelings, he said, "Discharge granted. Note for the record that Dr. Piper has enjoyed a long and prestigious career in Starfleet. All of us who have served alongside him on the *Enterprise* for the last year tender the doctor our gratitude and respect for a job well done . . . and our best wishes for a fruitful retirement."

"Duly noted," Spock assured him, entering the sentiment into the record for posterity. Then he consulted his list again.

The Vulcan didn't go on immediately, however. Studying him, the captain wondered about that.

"Don't tell me we're done already," he said at last.

Spock shook his head. "No, sir. There is one more transfer request." He looked up at Kirk. "From Lieutenant Hikaru Sulu."

The captain felt as if he had been blindsided by a rampaging bull. Sulu was one of his most dedicated and trusted officers, and had been since the *Enterprise* set out from Earth's solar system more than a year earlier. Kirk had always believed the astrophysics chief was happy and fulfilled doing his job on the ship.

"Are you sure?" the captain asked.

"I am quite sure," the first officer replied. "The

lieutenant has asked for a transfer to another Constitution-class vessel."

Kirk shook his head. "I don't get it."

Had he missed something? Why would Sulu, of all people, ask for a transfer to another starship?

"We'll get to the bottom of this," the captain promised himself. He reached for the monitor and pressed a square silver stud built into its base. "Mr. Sulu," he said, "this is Captain Kirk."

The response wasn't a moment in coming. "Sulu here."

"I'm in the briefing room with Mr. Spock," the captain told him. "I'd like you to join us here immediately."

A pause. "Right away, sir," said Sulu.

Kirk glanced at Spock and sat back in his chair, feeling more than a little discomfited. Under different circumstances, perhaps, he might have been able to take Sulu's request in stride. Under *these* circumstances, he found it a lot more difficult.

The captain had just lost his best friend, for godsakes. And Kelso as well, not to mention Dr. Dehner and nine other crewmen—all casualties of the *Enterprise*'s encounter with the galaxy's edge. Before long, he would say goodbye to Piper too. He couldn't stand the idea of losing anyone else.

Before long, the door panel slid aside and Sulu walked into the room. The astrophysicist was a slender man with dark hair and eyes, prominent cheekbones, and a ready smile. At the moment, however, he wasn't smiling.

Sulu inclined his head in Kirk's direction, then the Vulcan's. "Captain," he said. "Mr. Spock."

"Have a seat," Kirk said unceremoniously. He gestured to one with the hand encased in the cast.

Sulu pulled out a chair and sat down.

"Mr. Spock tells me you've requested a transfer," the captain began. "Is this true?"

The lieutenant nodded. "It is, sir."

"And what, may I ask, is the reason for it?"

Sulu didn't answer right away. "I . . . probably should have discussed it with you first," he told the captain.

"Not just probably, Lieutenant, but we'll set that aside for the moment. What I want to know is . . ." He spread his hands in an appeal for reason. "Why, Hikaru? I thought you liked it here."

Sulu frowned. "I do."

"Then why leave?" Kirk pressed.

The man took a breath and let it out. "Sir . . . I know I never said anything about it, but I've been bored for a very long time."

The captain's eyes widened in surprise. "Bored, Lieutenant? Of serving on the *Enterprise?*"

"Bored of serving in astrophysics," Sulu told him. "I mean, I found the subject absorbing at the Academy, and no less so when I went out into space. But . . ." He shrugged. "No disrespect to my colleagues here or at the Academy, sir, but I'm no longer fascinated."

Kirk tapped his fingers on the table in front of him. "I see," he said, sensing there was more the lieutenant wanted to say. "And if astrophysics doesn't fascinate you, what does?"

"Well," said Sulu, warming visibly to the subject, "I've been qualified to serve at the helm for some time now."

"The helm?" Kirk blurted.

"Yes, sir," the lieutenant told him. "That's why I asked for a transfer to another ship. I thought I'd have a better chance of becoming helmsman on a newly commissioned vessel."

I should have seen this coming, the captain told himself. *I should have realized something was up.*

But he hadn't. Distracted by other considerations, he had let Sulu's helm qualification pass under his nose without taking any notice of it. And now, he was about to pay the price for his oversight.

Obviously, it was his week for paying prices.

But, as luck would have it, there was a solution. After all, the *Enterprise* had an opening for a helmsman these days. The funeral Kirk had just attended had made that painfully obvious.

He tendered the offer. Sulu absorbed the implications for a moment, then lowered his eyes. "Mr. Kelso would be a tough act to follow," he said. "I don't know if I'm up to that."

The captain nodded. "I understand how you feel, Lieutenant. We all thought the world of Lieutenant Kelso. On the other hand, I don't want a stranger coming in to pilot the *Enterprise,* which is what'll happen if you decline the position. And frankly, I can't think of anyone Kelso would rather see follow in his footsteps than you."

Sulu blushed a little. "When you put it that way, sir, it's difficult to say no."

"That's the idea," Kirk confessed. "So . . . will you do it?"

The physicist took a moment to think about it. Finally, he nodded. "I'd be honored to, sir."

The captain extended his hand, cast and all. Sulu clasped it gratefully.

"Thank you," said the new helmsman.

"Thank *you,*" Kirk told him. "And now that that's settled, I should tell you that you'll be paired with a new navigator. A Lieutenant David Bailey, formerly of the *Potemkin.* He comes to us highly recommended, but he'll need someone to show him the way we do things around here."

"It'll be my pleasure," the lieutenant assured him.

Kirk smiled. "I had a feeling you'd say that."

But if Sulu had a tough act to follow, Bailey's challenge would be doubly difficult. After all, his predecessor was Gary Mitchell.

Sulu got up from his chair. "I'll let everyone in astrophysics know what's going on." He paused. "Incidentally, sir, if you want my recommendation for a new section head . . ."

"Who would that be?" the captain asked.

"Tammy O'Shea," said Sulu. "She's got the experience and the respect of her colleagues. I think she'd do fine."

Kirk nodded. "I'll take that under consideration, Lieutenant. Now get going. Your shift at helm starts in a couple of hours."

Sulu grinned. "Aye, sir. Thank you again, sir." He inclined his head to Spock. "You too, Commander," he told the Vulcan.

Then he left the briefing room, as satisfied as a man could be. The captain couldn't help chuckling as he watched Sulu go.

"He was pleased," Spock observed.

"That he was," Kirk agreed. He glanced at his first officer. "That's it, then, Mr. Spock? We've covered everything?"

"We have," said the Vulcan. "You already know about Mr. Bailey and the other newcomers from our previous discussions."

He started to turn off the monitor.

"Don't," said the captain.

Spock looked at him. "Sir?"

"I want to go over their files again," Kirk explained. "The newcomers, I mean. Get to know them a little better before they arrive."

"As you wish," the first officer replied. He got up to go, then paused just shy of the threshold and turned around again. "Sir," he said, "if you feel the need to speak of Lieutenant Mitchell again . . ."

The captain held his cast-covered hand up. "That's all right, Spock. I appreciate the offer, but it's not necessary. Really."

To show the Vulcan he wasn't lying, he smiled. Spock seemed to accept that as a token of his sincerity.

"Very well," said the first officer. He exited the room without another word, leaving Kirk all alone.

The captain turned to the monitor in the center of the table, which continued to display Sulu's personnel file. Leaning forward, he used the controls at the base of the monitor to open a new file—that of Lieutenant

David Bailey, who would replace Gary at the navigation console.

Bailey had an impressive set of credentials, no question about it. At twenty-four, only two years out of the Academy, he had already earned himself a couple of medals and a set of lieutenant's bands, along with a sparkling recommendation from the captain of the *Carolina.*

In fact, he reminded the captain a bit of himself at that age. Kirk, too, had come with more than his share of accolades.

Of course, Bailey would need more than credentials and recommendations to win the trust of his colleagues. He would have to show them what he was made of. He would have to prove himself in a tight spot before they would consider him one of their own.

The captain grunted softly. After all, no one knew what it took to become an officer better than he did.

With Bailey's background fresh in his mind again, Kirk closed the man's file and opened another one. Leaning back in his chair, he considered the dark-skinned beauty whose image smiled back at him from the monitor, her expression and her bearing charged with confidence and enthusiasm.

As the captain recalled, the woman's name was a difficult one to remember. But then, he was the one who had confused Smith with Jones.

"Let's see," he said, not wanting to make that particular mistake a second time. "You would be . . ." With some care, he read the name below the picture. "Ah, that's right. Lieutenant Uhura."

Chapter Three

Captain's Personal Log, supplemental.

It's been six days since we left Delta Vega, but I still feel hollowed out with grief. I see my friend Gary all too frequently in my dreams, reaching out to me, begging me to spare his life—or taking mine in some ghastly turnaround of circumstances. I try to tell myself that these nightmares won't go on forever—that, at some point, I'll be able to put the events of Gary's death behind me. After all, I've dealt with tragedy before.

SITTING IN HIS captain's chair, Kirk watched Starbase 33 loom larger and larger on his forward viewscreen. One of the latest facilities built by the Federation, the station resembled a child's top, its wide, circular body tapering to what looked like a point at its bottom.

No doubt it would be well equipped inside. It would have its share of specialty restaurants and shops, gymnasiums and rec lounges, theaters and botanical gardens. It would be a pleasant enough place to enjoy a well-deserved shore leave.

But there wouldn't be any shore leave there for Kirk's crew. Not this time, at least. He had made the trip for business, not pleasure.

"All stop," he said.

"Aye, sir," Alden responded from the helm as he worked to disengage the impulse engines. "All stop."

The insectlike drone of the ship's engines, always present, diminished. It made it that much easier to hear the bridge's other sounds—the beeping of its consoles, the soft footfalls and muted conversation of its personnel.

Dezago swiveled in his seat at the communications console. "They're hailing us, sir."

"On screen," said the captain.

A moment later, he saw the image of the starbase supplanted by that of an attractive, blond-haired junior officer. A full lieutenant, judging by the bands on the woman's uniform.

"Welcome to Starbase Thirty-three, sir." The woman somehow seemed cheerful and businesslike at the same time.

Kirk nodded. "Thank you, Lieutenant . . . ?"

"Willoughby, sir. Mariah Willoughby," the woman informed him. "Admiral Saylor's attaché. The admiral's informed me that he would like to see you at your earliest convenience."

"I'm heading for my transporter room now," the captain said. "Tell the admiral I shouldn't be more than a few minutes."

"I'll make the necessary arrangements with your transporter officer," the lieutenant assured him. "Willoughby out."

The woman disappeared, giving way to the image of the station. Kirk turned to his first officer.

"You've got the conn," he told Spock.

"Aye, sir," the Vulcan replied, leaving his science station to move to the center seat.

Out of habit, the captain took a quick look around to make sure everything was in good hands. It was, of course. Spock was a very capable commander and each bridge station was manned by a veteran operator.

Satisfied, Kirk headed for the turbolift. When the doors slid open in front of him, he entered the narrow lift compartment and punched in his destination. To the accompaniment of a high, shrill tone of increasing intensity, the lift began to move. The captain took a deep breath and waited to be deposited in the corridor outside the transporter room.

Debriefings, he thought. At best, they were a tedious and time-consuming activity. At times like this, when a mission had been marred by frustration and loss, they could be downright painful.

Still, Kirk recognized the need to conduct them. True, every starship sent out by the Fleet was outfitted with a sophisticated set of sensors—but the keenest data-gathering devices on board were the eyes, ears, and minds of its crew. No picture could be complete, no information thoroughly comprehended, without the crew's sentient input.

As the captain thought that, the high, shrill tone diminished and the door to the turbolift opened, giving him access to the corridor outside. Exiting the lift, he turned left and headed for the ship's only transporter room.

The doors to the place slid aside at his approach, revealing a man with lean features and straw-colored hair dressed in red-orange duty togs. The fellow turned away from his console and nodded to him.

"Good to see you, sir," said Lieutenant Kyle.

"Same here," Kirk responded. *Though I wish it were under different circumstances,* he added silently.

Crossing the room, the captain stepped up onto the transporter platform, as he had a hundred times since the *Enterprise* left Earth more than a year earlier. Then he turned to face Kyle.

"Ready when you are," he told the technician.

"Aye, Captain," said Kyle, his fingers darting across his controls with practiced ease. "Everything's set, mind you. I'm just waiting for the base to lower her shields so we can proceed."

Kirk sighed. Part of him wanted to get this over with and be on his way again. But another part of him wanted to linger at the starbase, no matter how uncomfortable he might find his time there.

After all, Gary's parents were waiting for him on Earth—depending on him to deliver the eulogy at their son's funeral. No doubt, being the type of people they were, they would embrace the captain as if he were the brother Gary had never had.

But how could he embrace the Mitchells in return? How could he speak to them or anyone else about his friend's death when Kirk was the one who had engineered it?

He remembered the way the trigger of the phaser rifle had felt against his finger, the way the winds had howled and driven bits of debris into his face as he raised the weapon to his eyes. He could see Gary hauling himself out of the grave he himself had excavated, confident and determined, ready to destroy the captain with a single gesture.

"Sir?" said Kyle. "We're ready now."

Kirk shivered as he was drawn forcibly from his reverie. He was holding his cast again, he noticed. "Energize," he told the lieutenant.

Kyle did as he was told. His console trilled, its red and green lights illuminating his features.

The captain didn't feel anything as his molecules were drawn into the transporter's pattern buffer, or as they were shot through space along an annular confinement beam and reorganized nearly half a kilometer away. He just knew suddenly that he was somewhere else.

In this case, that "somewhere else" was the starbase's transporter facility, which was a good deal more spacious and comfortable-looking than the one on the *Enterprise*. Of course, Kirk reflected, it could afford to be. The station didn't have to push itself all over the galaxy.

Lieutenant Willoughby, who had welcomed the captain to the base's environs on his viewscreen, was present to welcome him in person as well. Nodding to the transporter operator to acknowledge a job well done, she advanced to the platform as Kirk stepped down.

"If you'll come with me, sir," she said, "the admiral is waiting in Briefing Room One."

The captain grunted. "It's nice to have so many briefing rooms you have to number them," he told her.

Willoughby smiled. "I suppose it is, sir."

With that, the lieutenant led him out of the transporter room and down a gently curving corridor. The ceilings, Kirk noted, were higher than those he had seen on other starbases. Apparently, headquarters was paying a little more attention to creature comforts these days.

A few moments later, the captain and his escort stopped in front of a set of double doors. The doors slid apart, revealing a long, angular space almost twice the size of the *Enterprise*'s briefing room.

There were two men inside. Kirk recognized one of them as Admiral Saylor, a tall, white-haired fellow with a thick mustache whom he had met a couple of years earlier at a Starfleet function in San Francisco. The other was a stocky, dark-haired man with a wide mouth, an overhanging brow, and captain's bands decorating his sleeves.

"Jim," said Saylor, coming around the table to greet him. He put his hand out, then saw the cast on

Kirk's wrist and tactfully withdrew the offer. "It's good to see you."

"It's good to see you, sir," the captain replied. He turned to the other man, whom he had never seen before.

The dark-haired man didn't extend his hand. Instead, he inclined his head ever so slightly. "Francis Damion," he said.

"Jim Kirk," the captain told him.

"Yes," Damion responded, without expression. "I know."

Kirk noticed a faint antiseptic smell in the room— the kind one usually found in a lab. It gave him the feeling he was about to be dissected like a frog in some twentieth-century biology class.

"As you can imagine," said the admiral, "Starfleet Command has been eager to hear the results of your mission, Jim. They've sent Captain Damion to conduct the debriefing."

Kirk glanced at Saylor, a little confused. "I thought that was your function, Admiral. After all, it was you who assigned us the mission."

The admiral looked vaguely apologetic. "Normally, of course, that would be the case," he conceded. "However, Command has decided to handle this situation a bit differently."

The captain turned to Damion. "I see."

The dark-haired man indicated the table beside them with a gesture. Like the one in the *Enterprise*'s briefing room, it had a three-sided monitor sitting in the center of it, though this device's screens were a bit larger than the ones Kirk was used to.

"Let's get the ball rolling," said Damion, "shall we?"

The captain shrugged. "Why not?"

As he sat down, he saw the other captain produce a data padd like the one Spock favored. At least, that was how it looked. Damion tapped some information into it, then laid it on the table.

A recording device, Kirk thought. Not unheard of in debriefings, but an unusual touch nonetheless. *Or should I say* another *unusual touch,* the captain remarked inwardly,

"You know," he said helpfully, "my communications officer is transmitting my pertinent captain's logs as we speak. I'm sure you'll find everything you need in them."

Damion smiled a humorless smile. "It's my job to be thorough," he explained. "I'm sure you understand."

Kirk smiled the same smile back at him. "Of course," he said.

But, clearly, the proceedings were becoming rather formal. The captain couldn't help feeling he was entering an interrogation instead of a debriefing— that he was going to be pumped for information by someone whose agenda wasn't necessarily the same as his own.

Life began to feel as if he and that twentieth-century lab frog had a fair amount in common.

"Now, then," Damion began, "as I understand it, you were contacted by Admiral Saylor fifteen days ago. He gave you new orders—to explore and even exceed the boundaries of our galaxy."

Kirk nodded. "That's correct. And, of course, we followed those orders to the letter."

"You reached the limits of our galaxy?" the dark-haired man asked.

"What we *think* of as our galaxy," the captain amended.

"Very well," said Damion, taking the amendment in stride. "And what did you find there?"

Kirk took a breath, let it out. He found he didn't like his interrogator much. "We were confronted by an energy barrier."

Saylor leaned forward, the wrinkles around his eyes deepening. "An energy barrier, you say? Did you actually see this barrier, Jim? Or did it simply turn up on your sensor grid?"

"We saw it," the captain told him. "It was large, pinkish in color. And bright—very bright. Even with our viewscreen filters in operation, it hurt my eyes to look at it."

"Then what?" Damion asked.

"It didn't seem to present any danger to the ship," Kirk explained, "so we tried to cross it—again, in accordance with the admiral's orders. It turned out to be a mistake."

Damion tilted his head slightly. "In what way?"

In what way? Kirk echoed inwardly. *In every way you can imagine,* he thought. But that wasn't what he said.

"When we came in contact with the barrier," he answered, "it became a lot more intense. A lot more tumultuous. It tossed us around violently, rendering our warp drive inoperative. More importantly, it caused a number of fatalities among the crew."

"How many?" asked Damion, though his question smacked more of curiosity than sympathy.

Kirk lifted his chin as he considered the question. "Nine members of my crew perished instantly as a result of injuries to their central nervous systems. Two others died some time later. One was Lieutenant Gary Mitchell, my primary helm officer. The second was Dr. Elizabeth Dehner, a psychiatrist who had joined us to study starship crew reactions under emergency conditions."

"Eleven altogether, then," Damion concluded. He might as well have been making out a shopping list, for all the emotion he showed. "And when, exactly, did Mitchell and Dehner succumb?"

The captain frowned at the man's choice of words. "They didn't. At least, not in the way you mean."

Damion's eyes narrowed. "Would you care to elaborate?" he asked, though it wasn't really a question.

Not really, thought Kirk. Unfortunately, it appeared he had little choice in the matter.

"Both Mitchell and Dehner were on the bridge when we encountered the energy barrier," he reported. "So were half a dozen other officers, myself included. Most of us were unaffected by the exposure, but Mitchell and Dehner"—he couldn't help cringing inside at the memory—"lit up like sparklers on the Fourth of July."

Saylor shook his head. "The Fourth of July . . . ?"

It wasn't the first time the captain had forgotten— not everyone in the Fleet had grown up on Earth, and many who *had* grown up there weren't all that well versed in American history.

"A national independence ritual in the old United States of America," Damion explained efficiently. "It was typically celebrated with gunpowder-based fireworks displays."

"That's the one," said Kirk.

The admiral nodded. "And you say these people . . . lit up?"

"That's correct," the captain told him. "They throbbed with energy, pulsated with it. If there's a better way to describe what happened, I can't think of it."

The dark-haired man considered the information. "And what effect did this have on them?" he asked.

"In Dr. Dehner's case," said Kirk, "it didn't seem to have any effect at all—once we disengaged from the barrier. Lieutenant Mitchell, on the other hand, complained of weakness. And . . ."

Damion's brow knit. "Yes, Captain?"

Kirk remembered how his stomach had tightened when he saw his friend stretched out on the deck beside the helm console. He remembered kneeling beside him, asking him how he was . . . turning him over as quickly as he could, so he could get a look at Gary's face.

And he remembered how shocked he was by what he saw there. "His eyes," the captain said, "had begun to glow."

"To glow?" Damion echoed, despite himself. He looked at Kirk askance. "You're exaggerating, I take it."

The captain shook his head slowly from side to side. "I wish I were. Mitchell's eyes were alight with some kind of energy I had never seen before." He swallowed. "It was an eerie sight, to say the least."

"I can imagine," said Admiral Saylor.

"And that was the only effect it had on him?" asked Damion.

Kirk looked at him. "No. After a while, I witnessed other changes. From time to time, his voice took on a weird, echoing quality. And he began reading at speeds none of us could believe."

Damion's eyes hardened. "You saw him do this?"

Kirk nodded. "And I wasn't the only one. My first officer and I were monitoring Mitchell from the bridge, tracking his behavior. What's more, Mitchell knew it."

"What do you mean?" asked Saylor.

"He sensed us watching him," the captain elaborated, a chill climbing his spine as he recalled the incident. "He turned around and smiled at us, the way an adult might smile at a curious child. That's when we started to understand what had happened on the *Valiant*."

Again, the admiral was at a loss. His frustration showed on his face. "And the *Valiant* was . . . ?"

"An Earth ship," Kirk explained, "that beat us to the galaxy's edge by some two hundred years. We found its communications buoy shortly before we discovered the energy barrier."

Saylor looked at Damion, surprised and intrigued if his expression was any indication. However, the dark-haired man didn't look back at him. "Please continue," Damion told the captain.

Kirk complied. "As it turned out," he said, "the *Valiant*'s experience was remarkably similar to our own. Though several of its crewmen were injured when it encountered the barrier, one of them managed to survive—just as Mitchell had survived."

He paused, remembering how tense Spock had seemed as he extracted the buoy's information, piece by piece. "Then something strange happened on the *Valiant*. Her captain began making inquiries about extrasensory perception—inquiries that became more and more urgent, more and more frantic as time went on. Finally, for no apparent reason, the man destoyed his own ship."

The admiral looked shocked—but not Damion. As usual, he didn't register any emotion at all.

"He destroyed it?" asked Saylor.

"Yes," Kirk confirmed.

"For no apparent reason, you say?"

"None we could determine," the captain told him. "At least, not from the communications buoy alone. But before long, we began to get an inkling of what might have led him to that act."

"And how did that come about?" Damion asked.

"As I noted," said Kirk, "the *Valiant*'s captain seemed to have become obsessed with extrasensory perception. With that in mind, my first officer decided to analyze the personnel records of our own people—especially those who had been injured by the energy barrier. What he found was that Lieutenant Mitchell had the highest esper quotient on the *Enterprise.* Dr. Dehner had the second-highest esper quotient."

"And," the admiral noted, "of all those affected by the barrier, they were the only two who survived."

The captain nodded. "The only two."

It had been an eerie realization, to say the least. It had felt as if the deck under his feet had turned to quicksand.

"Then the *Valiant* crewman," said Saylor, "the one who was injured and survived . . . you think he could have been an esper as well?"

"That would explain his captain's preoccupation with the subject," Kirk told him.

The admiral regarded him. "And his decision to destroy his ship . . . had something to do with that crewman as well?" He seemed to be at a loss again. "Is that the conclusion you and your first officer came to?"

The captain sighed. "Allow me to apologize, sir. I didn't mean to get ahead of myself."

"But that *is* what you and your exec were thinking," Damion concluded, his eyes bright with curiosity. "That this crewman on the *Valiant* was the cause of his captain's drastic action."

"That's what we were thinking," Kirk confirmed. He looked at Admiral Saylor. "You have to understand, sir, Lieutenant Mitchell was changing rapidly. And I'm not just talking about his eyes, or his voice, or the remarkable speed at which he read."

"Then what?" asked the admiral.

The captain frowned. "He was becoming something more than human—something that could shut down its own vital signs at will. And then start them again. Or even make subtle adjustments in the ship's operating systems."

Saylor didn't seem ready to accept such events. "Jim, if you're taking liberties with the truth here . . ."

"It's all in my report," Kirk assured him. "Every word of it."

Damion scowled—the first small sign of emotion that he had shown since the debriefing began. "Let him go on, sir," he told the admiral.

Saylor grumbled, but did as the dark-haired man suggested. "Let's hear the rest," he said.

The captain recalled the way Gary had lain in his biobed, his eyes ablaze with that weird, silver light. His friend had seemed so distant, so terribly aloof from everyone. Now, of course, Kirk knew why.

Gary had been reaching into himself. He had been exploring the breathtaking depth of his burgeoning powers. And no one except Gary himself had had any idea of what he was up to.

"Of course," Kirk said as dispassionately as he could, "none of these developments necessarily constituted a reason to fear the man." He eyed Saylor, then Damion. "I should point out at this juncture that Lieutenant Mitchell was my friend—my best friend—and I had always trusted him implicitly. It was difficult for me to think of him as a menace to my ship or crew."

"But you were wrong," the dark-haired man suggested.

"I was wrong," the captain admitted.

So *very* wrong.

"And your officers?" Damion wondered. "What did they think of the changes in Lieutenant Mitchell?"

Kirk shrugged. "Dr. Dehner was even less wary of him than I was—though I realized later that she was attracted to him, and might not have been looking at the situation objectively. But Mr. Spock, my first officer . . . he saw right through to the truth."

"Which was?" asked the admiral, eager to hear it straight out.

The captain took a breath, then let it out. "That Mitchell was evolving into something that would soon have little or nothing in common with us," he answered reluctantly. "That he was becoming a serious threat to the *Enterprise* and everyone on her."

Kirk remembered the intensity of his argument with the Vulcan, recalling the way they had laid into each other with their words. "Spock reasoned that we had two choices if we were to avoid the fate of the *Valiant*—kill Lieutenant Mitchell outright or strand him on an unpopulated world." Even now, he could feel the awful weight of that decision. "I chose the latter."

"You decided to abandon your friend?" asked Damion.

It sounded to Kirk like an accusation. "I had no choice," he told the dark-haired man between clenched teeth. "It was either him or the other four hundred and ten people on the *Enterprise.*"

The room was silent for a moment. Then, bit by bit, the captain regained control of himself.

"The nearest unpopulated world," he said, "was

Delta Vega—a planet with a lithium-cracking facility."

"I know it," Saylor replied. "A stark, forbidding place."

Kirk nodded sadly. He recalled how guilty he felt—how it tore him up inside to leave his friend in such a hellish environment.

"When we got there," he went on, "Mitchell seemed to know where we were and what we were planning. Nonetheless, we managed to catch him unaware. We sedated him, beamed down to the surface with him, and imprisoned him behind a high-intensity forcefield. Then we borrowed what we needed from the planet's lithium-processing equipment."

"Borrowed?" the admiral echoed.

"When we tried to cross the energy barrier," the captain reminded him, "we lost our warp drive. The only way we could repair it was to strip the facility's backup systems."

"So you were killing two birds with one stone," Damion observed.

Again, Kirk thought, the man's choice of words left something to be desired. "You might say that," he answered in the same cold tone.

"But you said Mitchell died eventually," Damion noted. "And Dehner as well. Or am I mistaken?"

"You heard it correctly," the captain told him.

"Under what circumstances did they die?" asked the dark-haired man.

Kirk eyed him. "That depends."

Damion returned the look. "On what?"

With his left hand, Kirk reached for the dark-haired man's data padd. Picking it up, he shut off its recording function. Then, as Damion and Admiral Saylor looked on, he set it down on the table again.

"It depends," he continued evenly, "on whether or not you still intend to record this conversation."

"And if I do?" asked the dark-haired man.

"Then Mitchell and Dehner died in the pursuit of their duty," Kirk told him, "and I don't care to go into any further detail."

The admiral looked at him in amazement. "You don't care . . . ?" he repeated, dumbfounded. "Do you know where you are, Jim?"

"I do indeed, sir," the captain assured him. "And I recognize my obligation to both you and the Fleet. However, I have an obligation to my people as well, and I won't say or do anything that will smear the good names of Gary Mitchell and Elizabeth Dehner."

Saylor scowled. "You were dispatched on a scientific mission—a mission eleven of your crewmen died to carry out. And now you're telling me you'd withhold the results of that mission?"

"Not at all," Kirk replied. "The scientific results are and will remain part of the official record, as entered in my logs. It's the other results I don't care to parade in public—the personal behaviors that took place, which have little or nothing to do with what we can learn from our encounter with the energy barrier."

"But you have no objection to discussing these behaviors off the record," Damion established.

The captain nodded. "That's correct."

The dark-haired man considered him for a moment. Then he said, "All right. I can live with that. Proceed, Captain Kirk."

No "please" this time, Kirk observed. But then, pleasantries were reserved for officers who were pliable—not those who dared to question Starfleet Command and its chosen representatives.

"As I told you," the captain went on, "we took what we needed from the lithium-processing equipment. But as we worked, Lieutenant Mitchell was continuing to change—continuing to grow stronger. Unbeknownst to myself and First Officer Spock, he reached out with the power of his mind and strangled one of my other officers with a cable."

Saylor winced.

"Then," said Kirk, plowing ahead, "he burst through the field that confined him, knocked the rest of us out, and took Dr. Dehner with him."

"My god," the admiral exclaimed. "That poor woman."

The captain didn't respond to the remark. He simply proceeded with his story, telling it as he saw fit.

"When I woke," Kirk continued, "I knew what I had to do. After all, it was my fault my friend had gotten so far. I left orders with my chief medical officer—if I didn't contact the ship in twelve hours, Spock was to break orbit and irradiate the planet with neutron beams."

"An extreme measure," Damion remarked.

"For an extreme situation," the captain responded. "Then I picked up a phaser rifle Spock had brought down with him, tucked it under my arm, and went after Lieutenant Mitchell."

"On your own?" asked Saylor.

"On my own," Kirk confirmed.

"Wasn't that ill-considered?" the admiral wondered. "A being powerful enough to break free of a forcefield—"

"Would be powerful enough to smear me all over the landscape," the captain said, finishing Saylor's thought for him. "True enough. But the odds of rescuing Dehner wouldn't have been any better if I had brought an army with me. I was hoping I could talk to Mitchell, reason with him. And if I couldn't, the only life I would be sacrificing was my own."

"A courageous gesture," Damion told him, though there was a hint of irony in his voice.

The admiral looked at him. "Captain Kirk is a courageous man."

The dark-haired man returned the look, but declined to make any other comments. Deriving a measure of satisfaction from the exchange, Kirk continued with his account.

"After a while," he said, "I found Dr. Dehner. I thought she would be at Mitchell's mercy, a mere pawn in his game—but as it turned out, I was wrong about that. You see, she had changed, too."

Saylor cursed colorfully beneath his breath. "She had the same powers you'd seen in Mitchell?"

"The same variety," the captain told him, "though she didn't appear to have the same command of them. In time, however, she would no doubt have become just as strong as he was—and just as aloof.

"I tried to enlist her help . . . appeal to what was left of her humanity. It wasn't easy, of course. Lieutenant Mitchell had already shown her the rewards of being on his side, which were staggering. But I planted some doubts in her mind, made her wary of him. I was starting to make some progress when Mitchell decided to join us."

Kirk remembered how it was. One second, there was no sign of his friend. The next, he was standing on a rocky ledge, his temples gray as if with age, his bearing even more regal than before.

No longer Gary. At least, that's what he had told himself at the time.

"I saw in Mitchell's eyes that there was no hope of reasoning with him," said the captain. "So I fired my phaser rifle at point-blank range—for all the good it did me. He disarmed me with a wave of his hand. Then, as if to show me how hopeless my position was, he dug a grave for me in the ground at his feet. He even made a headstone for it."

The admiral shook his head in amazement. Damion just looked at him, clearly more interested than impressed.

"Then," Kirk went on, "just when it looked as if my luck had run out, Dehner helped me after all. She sent a bolt of energy at Mitchell. He staggered and sent a bolt back at her. She attacked again; he counterattacked. And back and forth it went, enough energy crackling through the air to tear a mountain in half."

He shivered as he thought of it. Despite the danger, despite everything that hung in the balance, he had been mesmerized by the spectacle. "In the end," he said, "the doctor was mortally wounded. She slumped back against the rock. But she had weakened him. She had given me a chance."

The captain shook his head ruefully. After all, this was the hardest part. "I took advantage of it as best I could," he recalled. "Mitchell and I struggled, hand to hand, but even in his weakened state he was a match for me." He held up his cast. "Somewhere along the line, he damaged my wrist. Eventually, we fell into the grave he dug for me. I was fortunate enough to climb out first and recover my rifle."

Saylor frowned beneath his mustache. "But didn't you say your phaser fire had no effect on him?"

"It didn't," Kirk agreed. "But I didn't fire at Lieutenant Mitchell. I fired at a hunk of rock he had loosened from the cliff face above us." He felt his throat tighten, but he finished his story. "The boulder fell on him, crushing the life out of him."

"Unbelievable," said the admiral.

The captain adjusted his cast again, but he remained silent. Even now, days later, the memory was an open wound, raw and bloody and hideously painful.

Damion pondered Kirk's words for a moment. Then he asked, "Are you certain you killed him?"

The question rankled—but it was a fair one, under the circumstances. "First Officer Spock scanned the area for life signs for some time after the incident. He didn't find any."

"You said Mitchell could suppress his biosigns," Damion reminded him, his eyes piercing and alert.

The captain nodded. "He could—but why would

he want to? What could he gain by pretending to be dead?"

Damion seemed to see the sense in that. In any case, he didn't press the point any further.

Kirk fixed the dark-haired man with his gaze. "Now let me ask you a question, Captain."

Damion looked at him. "I beg your pardon?"

Kirk leaned forward. "Tell me . . . why is it you didn't seem surprised when I told you about the energy barrier we encountered?"

The lines in Damion's face hardened, but he didn't answer.

"Or when I described the message buoy launched by the *Valiant?*" Kirk asked. "Or the information we gleaned from it?"

Still no answer.

"Is it possible you knew about the barrier already?" Kirk persisted. "And about the buoy and maybe even the fate of the *Valiant?* Is that why my mentioning them didn't mean anything to you?"

Damion shook his head, his expression giving away nothing. "I'm not the one being debriefed here, Captain."

"Maybe not," Kirk conceded. "But still, I'd like my questions answered. If my crew and I have been used as guinea pigs, the least you can do is give me the courtesy of admitting it."

"Jim," said Saylor, "Damion's right. He's the one asking the questions here." But the admiral's expression told Kirk that he wouldn't mind hearing some answers himself.

The dark-haired man regarded Kirk for what

seemed like a long time. At last, he nodded. "All right, Captain. As long as we're speaking off the record . . . we did know about the *Valiant*. That is, we knew that it had been lost in that part of space some two hundred years ago. But I assure you, we didn't know the manner in which it had been lost, or that it represented a danger to any of your crewmen."

"Why wasn't I told about it anyway?" Kirk wondered. "Why wasn't I at least warned that another ship had gone that way?"

Damion didn't flinch. "The *Valiant*'s situation was classified," he said, "for reasons I can't go into. Information was available on a need-to-know basis only—and Command didn't believe you needed to know."

Kirk didn't like the man's answer. He didn't like it at all. But he knew he could find it in himself to accept it.

He had learned over the years that, even as a starship captain, he wouldn't be privy to everything in Starfleet's files. Certain kinds of data would be denied to him. This was just one more annoying example of it.

"Keep in mind," the dark-haired man continued, "after you discovered the *Valiant*'s communications buoy, you had more data than we did—and it didn't change your decision one iota. You still didn't deem the situation dangerous enough to turn away from the energy barrier."

Kirk frowned. "There's a difference, Captain. When I ask my people to put their lives on the line, I don't pull any punches. I don't withold potentially important information from them."

"You're honest with them," Damion noted.

"Damned right," the captain confirmed.

"You can afford to be," the dark-haired man observed. "You're only their captain. You're not Starfleet Command."

Chapter Four

NURSE CHRISTINE CHAPEL looked up from the biobed where she had been running a diagnostic routine for the last several minutes. Across the breadth of the *Enterprise*'s wide, pastel-colored sickbay, Chief Medical Officer Mark Piper was sitting alone in his office, going through some of the many personal items he had gathered for packing.

Chapel recognized a few of them. For instance, the stone carving of a big-bellied Baliba'an fertility goddess. It had been given to the doctor by some Oritixx traders he had healed after they narrowly survived the explosion of their merchant vessel.

Not that Piper had had any serious need of the goddess's services. With four sons, a daughter, and more than fifteen grandchildren, the man had done fine before making her acquaintance.

Then there was the latinum honor medallion he had received on Cerebus Prime, where he had saved millions by discovering a cure for Hiinkan Plague. The last the nurse had heard, the Hiinkans were naming their third new medical center after the doctor.

The last memento was a primitive dart—the one Piper had removed from Lieutenant Mitchell after he and the captain were ambushed by native hunters on Dimorus. It had been touch and go for the lieutenant for a while, but the doctor had finally pulled him through.

And now Mitchell was dead, despite everything, she thought. Dead and buried on a lonely planetoid far from the beaten track. It was funny the way life worked. Funny . . . and often unbearably tragic.

The nurse checked the biobed and saw that the diagnostic was complete. As it happened, the bed was in perfect condition. Noting that on her padd, she crossed sickbay and joined Piper at his desk.

The chief medical officer looked up at her. "Just going through a few things," he explained a bit awkwardly, his eyes uncharacteristically liquid beneath bushy, dark brows.

Chapel smiled. "I can see that."

Piper looked around. "I don't know . . . I guess I'll miss this place, Christine. But most of all," he told her, "I'll miss you. You've been one hell of an associate."

The nurse nodded, trying desperately to keep a rein on her emotions. "Thanks," she replied. "I couldn't have asked for anyone better than you either. I just hope . . .”

“Yes?” the doctor asked.

Chapel shrugged. “I just hope whoever replaces you is half the physician you are.”

That brought some color to Piper's cheeks. “Well,” he said, “now you've done the impossible, Christine. You've made an old man blush.”

The nurse regarded him for a moment. “No,” she told him. “It's you who've done the impossible, Doctor, more times than I care to count. And I'm going to miss you very, very much.”

Unable to control herself any longer, she gave the chief medical officer a hug—the kind she never would have given him while there was still the prospect of their working together. What's more, Piper hugged her back, the way he might have hugged one of his granddaughters.

Finally, he released her. “Go ahead,” he told Chapel. “Finish what you were doing. I don't want the next doctor to curse me for leaving him with a bunch of temperamental biobeds.”

The nurse straightened. “Of course not,” she agreed. Then she swallowed back the lump in her throat, crossed sickbay again, and initiated the diagnostic routine for the next biobed.

Things aren't going to be the same around here, she told herself. *No matter who his replacement is.*

Dr. Leonard McCoy sat in front of the surgeon general's desk, peered out the man's floor-to-ceiling window at the gulls wheeling over the undulating waves of the blue Pacific, and said, "Damn the Capellans. Damn 'em all to hell."

If McCoy listened closely, he could hear the squawking of the gulls through the plexiglass. What did *they* have to complain about? he wondered. They were only birds, and Terran birds at that. For godsakes, they hadn't even heard of the Capellans.

The doctor's gaze was drawn to the surface of the rounded, black desk. There, between his monitor and some pictures of his family, the surgeon general kept a small jar full of Vertigranen incense clusters—little, purple grapelike things that, when popped open, gave the air the honeyed smell of a Vertigranen rainforest in spring bloom.

"So," said a rich baritone voice from behind him, "how did you like your little mission on Capella Four?"

McCoy turned in his chair and saw the balding, stoop-shouldered figure of Harris Eggleton fill the doorway behind him. Eggleton, who had served as the highest-ranking official at Starfleet Medical for the last seven years, was McCoy's immediate superior.

"How did I like it?" asked the younger man, as Eggleton laid a meaty hand on his shoulder en route to his chair. "I didn't, that's how. The Capellans have got to be the stubbornest, orneriest, most backward people in the universe."

"Why do you say that?" asked the surgeon general, depositing his big, unwieldy frame into his over-stuffed, black chair.

McCoy grunted disapprovingly. "Here I am, ready to improve every aspect of their miserable lives with

Federation medical science, and what do they tell me? They're not interested. Why's that? I ask, dumbfounded. Because, they say, only the strong are meant to survive."

"And you think that's hogwash?" Eggleton suggested.

"You're not kidding I think it's hogwash! Why in blazes did the Capellans agree to have us beam down in the first place if they were going to ignore everything we had to offer?"

The surgeon general scratched his sparsely covered head and smiled to himself. "As I understand it, Leonard, they didn't ignore everything—just our medical technology."

McCoy jabbed a finger at his superior. "And that's just what those blockheads needed the most. Do you have any idea what the infant mortality is on that planet?"

"Sixteen percent, I believe," Eggleton replied. "But that doesn't mean the Capellans are going to do anything about it. They're stuck in their ways, just like a lot of cultures."

McCoy didn't comment. He just fumed.

"Frustrating," said the older man, "isn't it? Makes you want to grab them by their shoulders and shake some sense into them."

McCoy nodded. "Exactly right." Of course, the Capellans were a lot bigger than he was, and shaking them wouldn't have been an easy task—but that was beside the point.

Eggleton shrugged. "To tell you the truth, that's why I decided to take this job at Starfleet Medical.

There's none of the mess you run into when you're dealing with alien cultures. None of the personalities, either. Here, the most contentious thing you have to deal with on a daily basis might be a cranky microbe."

The younger man looked at him, taking note of the man's ulterior motive. "In other words, Doctor, you're saying I'd have to be a lunatic to go back out into space."

"Hey," said the surgeon general, "your words, not mine. I've made no secret of how much I want you to stay here and put your talents to good use. I mean, you *are* the fellow who created the technique we use for establishing axonal pathways between grafted neural pathways and basal ganglia . . . or am I thinking of a different Leonard H. McCoy?"

McCoy blushed. "Stop it. You're embarrassing me."

Eggleton looked him in the eye. "I'll stop embarrassing you, Leonard. But I won't stop arguing that all this planet-hopping isn't for you. At least, not at this point in your career."

McCoy frowned. From the age of twenty-six, when he joined the Fleet, he had been stationed on any number of alien worlds. He had even served as assistant chief medical officer on a starship for a while.

Then his father had fallen ill with a rare disease and he had asked for a transfer to Earth. He was told he could serve under Eggleton at Starfleet Medical in San Francisco, and his father would be transferred to a local facility, so he could keep an eye on the old man.

It was the worst time of McCoy's life. His father

went downhill quickly, but somehow he stopped short of actually dying. Instead, he lay there in his biobed, his sunken chest laboring pitifully as a respirator pumped in breath after breath, comatose but technically still alive.

Faced with subjecting his father to a lingering, painful death, McCoy had made the decision to take him off life support and watched him die—only to see a cure for the old man's disease discovered a few weeks later. The irony of it nearly shattered him.

In the end, he managed to cope, but only by clinging to familiar things. Starfleet Medical was one of them. And even after McCoy got past the worst of his father's death, even after he regained his equilibrium, it seemed easier to remain in San Francisco at the age of thirty-eight than to take the initiative and find a berth on a starship.

He hadn't sought out the Capella IV assignment. It had simply fallen into his lap. But the prospect of going out into space again had excited him, and the doctor had accepted the mission with great optimism . . . an optimism that had barely beamed down to the planet's surface before it was dashed by the obstinacy of the natives. *So much for the romance of the frontier,* he had thought at the time.

"I'll tell you what," said Eggleton. "Take the day off, all right? Work off some of that frustration in the gym or in the pool or however you like. Then show up here tomorrow, refreshed and renewed, and we can get started on that choriomeningitis vaccine."

McCoy worked up a smile. "Thanks," he replied,

"but I'd rather get started right away. No time like the present and all that."

The surgeon general nodded approvingly. "Whatever you say, Doctor. Far be it from me to stand in the way of progress."

The younger man stood. "See you later, then."

"Absolutely," said Eggleton.

As McCoy left the man's office, he found he was glad to get back to work. Real work, he remarked inwardly, not some glorified baby-sitting assignment. At Starfleet Medical, he made real discoveries. He furthered the cause of science in measurable ways.

His boss was right, he told himself, as he walked down a long, well-lit corridor to his own office. He was too set in his ways to go back to deep-space exploration. He had found his niche there on Earth.

In a way, the doctor thought, it was good he had made the trip to Capella IV. Otherwise, he might have wondered if he had made the wrong decision about staying on Earth. He might have wound up with doubts he would never have had a chance to dispel.

Suddenly, something occurred to him. Was it possible, he wondered, that Eggleton had sent him to the Capellans because he thought McCoy was getting an itch to move on? Was it possible the surgeon general had known just how annoying the assignment would be to his star research biologist—and that was exactly why he gave it to him?

As McCoy pondered the possibility, he turned and entered his office. It had a nice window, but nothing as expansive as Eggleton's, and it faced the city skyline instead of the ocean. His desk was smaller and more functional, and the air didn't contain even a hint of Vertigranen incense.

But it was his. It was familiar.

It was *home,* for petesakes.

As always, he glanced at his personal monitor screen, to see if there were any messages for him. There were several, as it turned out.

The first one was from Joanna, his daughter. A teenager now, she was on a skiing vacation in Wyoming with her friends, and she wanted him to know she was having a good time.

The doctor sighed. He wished he could have been a bigger part of Joanna's life when she was younger. But her mother had broken his heart so badly, he had spent most of the girl's earliest years in space, running away from a life that had spiraled out of his control.

The next four communications were from various colleagues asking McCoy for help or advice regarding their respective projects. He scanned them quickly to see what they wanted, then stored the messages until he had gone over the others in the queue.

A sixth missive was from a woman the doctor had been seeing. She wanted to know if he cared to escort her to a cocktail party on Alcatraz, even though the two of them weren't exactly an item anymore. He sent back an emphatic "No, thank you, ma'am."

McCoy hated cocktail parties—almost as much as he hated transporters, in fact. If the woman had paid a little more attention to him while they were going out, she might have known that. It was no wonder their relationship hadn't gone anywhere.

Then came the seventh message, which was a lot more of a surprise than any of the others. It was from Jim Kirk, with whom the doctor had served on the *Constitution* several years earlier.

Kirk was captain of the *Enterprise* now, and had been for over a year. His navigator was Gary Mitchell, a brash but entertaining young man whom McCoy had also met on the *Constitution*.

Kirk and the doctor corresponded every so often, but never twice in the same month—and they had spoken only a few weeks ago, when the captain had gotten wind of his friend's mission to Capella IV. So what was so blasted important that Kirk had seen fit to break with tradition?

McCoy frowned as he stared at the captain's name on the screen. He had a bad feeling about Kirk's message, somehow, a sense that he wouldn't like what he found in it. But that was silly, wasn't it?

Kirk could have been calling to say he had fallen in love or made first contact with a previously unknown species. He could have been calling to tell his friend that he had discovered an alien paradise—or better yet, a lifetime supply of Romulan ale.

There was a whole universe full of things the captain could have sent a message about, and they weren't all bad by a long shot. But as the doctor opened the file and read the communication, he realized it was bad.

It was very bad.

Leaning back in his chair, McCoy drew a ragged breath and tried to cope with what he had just read.

"Gary . . ." he said softly. "Lord, man . . . what did you do to yourself?"

Captain Damion's comment was still ringing in Kirk's ears as he made his way back to Starbase 33's transporter room, closely escorted by the ever-attentive Lieutenant Willoughby.

You're only their captain, Damion had told him smugly and unemotionally. *You're not Starfleet Command.*

Kirk swore beneath his breath. Only their captain indeed. Who did the man think he was?

Willoughby turned to him. "Did you say something, sir?"

The captain shook his head. "No, Lieutenant. Nothing."

It wasn't that Kirk had any illusions of absolute autonomy, even on his own starship. Regardless of the circumstances, he was always aware of the fact that he reported to a higher authority.

But as commanding officer of the *Enterprise,* he shared a relationship with his crew that the brass back in San Francisco had no role in. When a crewman was asked to risk his life, it was Kirk who did the asking. When a crewman was asked to kill, it was Kirk who took responsibility for it. And when a crewman died, it was Kirk who bore the guilt.

Not Starfleet. *Him.*

"Sir?" said Willoughby.

The captain glanced at her. "Yes, Lieutenant?"

He expected her to say something about how nice it was to meet him, or how much she hoped he had enjoyed his visit. But the woman didn't say anything like that. What she did was ask a question.

"Can you give me any advice, sir?" Willoughby inquired. "About serving on a starship, I mean?"

"Advice?" he echoed, caught off balance.

"Yes, sir," she responded. "You see, I'm shipping out on the *Defiant* the middle of next week."

Kirk nodded. "I see." He gave the matter some thought. "As I recall," he told Willoughby, "Captain Serling is commanding the *Defiant* these days. He's a no-nonsense type of commander. He doesn't like to see anyone deviate from the rules—especially someone who's new to his ship."

The lieutenant looked grateful for the tip. "Thank you, sir. I'll be sure to remember that," she told him. But as they proceeded down the corridor, she began to frown.

"Problem?" asked the captain.

Willoughby sighed. "To tell you the truth, sir, I thought I would be excited to take this posting. After all, I've been campaigning for it for several months now."

"But?" said Kirk.

The lieutenant shrugged. "I guess I've got a few butterflies. I mean, it's my first time on a starship, outside of a couple of Academy training missions. What if I start out on the wrong foot? I've heard of people who ran into a problem or two whose careers never recovered."

The captain shook his head. "The surest way to find yourself with a problem is to spend your time worrying about it. If I were you, Willoughby, I'd concentrate on doing the best job I can . . . and leave it at that."

He could see her filing the advice away for future reference. "I'll remember that too," the lieutenant promised him.

The transporter room was looming up ahead. Together, Kirk and Willoughby entered and nodded to the technician on duty.

"Captain Kirk will be returning to the *Enterprise* now," the lieutenant told the man behind the console, though he had no doubt already been notified of the captain's departure.

"Aye, sir," the operator replied, and made a few last-minute adjustments in his control settings. "Ready, sir," he told Kirk.

The captain took his position on the transporter platform. "Best of luck," he told Willoughby.

She smiled. "I appreciate that, sir."

He turned to the technician. "Energize."

A moment later, Kirk found himself in the smaller, more modestly furnished and eminently more familiar environs of the *Enterprise*'s transporter room. Lieutenant Kyle, who was standing behind the control console, looked up from his panel to acknowledge the captain's appearance.

"Welcome back, sir," he said.

"Thank you," Kirk told him.

Then he headed out the door and into the corridor. A turbolift ride later, he found himself emerging onto the ship's bridge, drawing glances from his command staff.

Their consoles were making shrill sounds as they worked, bright orange graphics flashing on their screens. And as always, there was the hum of the engines, more subdued now with the propulsion drives disengaged.

Home, the captain thought.

Spock, who was sitting in the center seat, gave it up when he saw Kirk coming. "Captain," he said.

"Mr. Spock," Kirk responded, as he sat down and made himself comfortable. "Anything to report?"

"Nothing out of the ordinary," said the Vulcan.

The captain hadn't expected there would be, in the short time he had been gone. He turned to Alden, who was sitting at the helm-navigation console next to Lieutenant Stiles.

"Heading one seven seven mark six," Kirk said, rattling off the numbers. "Full impulse, Lieutenant."

"Aye, sir," Alden responded.

Next, the captain glanced at his navigator. "Chart a course for Earth," he told Stiles.

"I've already begun, sir," responded Stiles, who had no doubt recognized the heading.

Spock looked at Kirk. "If you have no further need of me, sir, I would like to check on the progress of my aeroponics experiments."

The captain signified his permission with a nod. After all, the Vulcan was the *Enterprise*'s chief science officer as well as his exec. "Go to it, Mr. Spock. Dismissed."

With his first officer heading for the turbolift, Kirk sat back in his chair and watched Starbase 33 slide off the bridge's main viewscreen as Alden brought the ship about. What he had been through with Damion and Admiral Saylor seemed to slide away as well.

But not Willoughby. A little uncertain of herself but desperate to do well, she stuck in his mind and wouldn't let go.

The captain knew why, too. Seven years earlier, he had been a young lieutenant himself, embarking on his first real mission. And he had had his share of problems, all right. Big problems, even bigger than any Willoughby might have envisioned.

For a while, they had threatened to overwhelm him, to crush any hope he had of a long, productive career. But fortunately for Kirk, he'd had a friend to see him past the rough spots. . . .

2257

His knees wobbly, his throat sore with mounting grief, twenty-four-year-old Jim Kirk knelt over the bloodless corpse of his colleague.

Just a few minutes earlier, it had housed the spirit of a security officer named Piniella, an energetic young woman from Barcelona with flashing, dark eyes and a deep, hearty laugh and a love of strong liqueurs. Now it was a dead thing, its skin ivory-white and cold to the touch, its eyes staring blankly at the fate that had overtaken it.

Clenching his teeth against a flood of emotion, Kirk cursed long and loud in the depths of his soul. Then, with clumsy fingertips, he drew Piniella's eyelids down over her eyes.

He looked around him and saw the other corpses that littered the floor of the corridor in either direction. There were seven or eight of them in all, each as cold and bone-white as Piniella, each one gaping at the last thing they had seen in the world of the living.

Kirk knew what it was because he had seen it, too. But, unlike Piniella and the others, he wasn't a limp, cold bag of bones, little more than a marker to show where a living being had been.

He was alive.

And that was the problem.

Numbly, as if in a dream, the lieutenant got up and advanced to the intercom station built into the bulkhead on his right. With a touch of his hand, he activated it.

"Kirk to Captain Garrovick," he said, his voice a rustling of leaves in a lonely autumn cornfield.

No answer.

"Kirk to Captain Garrovick," he repeated, a little louder this time.

Still no response.

He tried the first officer next. Then the second officer, and the third. The results were the same each time. No one answered. All he heard when he called out each name was the ghostly hum of the engines and the twanging echo of his voice.

"Damn," the lieutenant shouted out loud, his stomach tightening so hard he could barely breathe.

He glanced at Piniella again. From where he stood, the security officer looked like something sculpted from blue-white limestone, something dressed in a Starfleet uniform as a macabre joke.

Were they all like that, Kirk wondered, every command officer on the *Republic?* Each one a husk drained of life and will and color, a porcelain puppet with its strings cut?

Then the enormity of it hit him. Maybe everyone was dead—not just the command staff, but every man and woman on the ship, every one of them an unsuspecting victim of the phenomenon that had assaulted them. Maybe, through some inexplicable twist of fortune, the lieutenant was the only survivor among the four hundred and twenty crewmen who had set out from Beta Trianguli five days earlier.

No, Kirk insisted. He couldn't stand it if that was the way it had happened. He couldn't—

"Lieutenant Kirk?" said a voice, echoing back on itself.

He turned to the intercom grid, his heart pounding. "Konerko?" he breathed. "Is that you?"

"Thank heaven," the ensign responded, her tone one of heartfelt relief. "I thought it had gotten you, too, sir."

"Where are you?" Kirk asked her.

"I'm on the bridge. But they're all dead here—the captain, Commander Tolan, Chief Smiley—everyone. I've taken the helm for the time being, but I'm not really qualified to—"

"Stay right there," he told her. "I'm on my way."

Negotiating a course through the shoals of his lifeless comrades, trying his best not to notice the wide-eyed rictus on their faces, the lieutenant made his way to the nearest turbolift on knees that threatened to betray him. A bend in the corridor showed him a new field of corpses, even more densely populated than the one he had left behind.

My god, he thought, his stomach coiling even tighter. *How can there be so many of them?*

As he advanced, putting one foot in front of the other, he realized with a start that his friend Gilhooley was lying among the dead. The man's merry blue eyes were rolled back in his head, his mouth yawning wide as if to drag in one last breath.

The day before, Kirk had played three-dimensional chess with Gilhooley in the ship's lounge and laughed at the man's off-color limericks. Now the poor bastard was a slab of meat rotting on the floor—no longer a person, but an empty husk.

It didn't seem real to the lieutenant. But then, how could it? How could anyone wrap his mind around the meaningless deaths of hundreds of his fellow human beings?

But that wasn't the worst of it. Not by a long shot, he thought. The worst part was the knowledge of how those deaths had taken place.

Swallowing hard, Kirk staggered on.

Eventually, he came in sight of the turbolift. As he reached it, his breath loud and strange-sounding in his ears, he fumbled with a computer pad set into the bulkhead. A moment later, the doors slid aside with a sigh and revealed the contents of the compartment.

There were two bodies inside. Kirk knew them—or

rather, knew who they had been in the world of the living. Hasegawa had hoped to be a chief engineer someday. Ojibwe had planned to get married when his tour was up. They would do neither of those things.

The lieutenant's throat threatened to close on him. *So much death,* he thought. *So many shattered hopes* . . .

Taking a deep, wheezing breath, he punched in the command that would halt the turbolift and keep its door open.

Then he entered the compartment and, as gently as he could, started to drag Ojibwe out into the corridor. He wasn't sure why he needed to do such a thing. He just knew that it had to be done.

"Sir?" came a strangely plaintive voice from behind him.

Dropping Ojibwe, Kirk whirled and reached for the wall of the compartment to support himself. But whatever he had pictured in his mind in that startled fraction of a second, he didn't find it.

It was only a couple of crewmen standing there—a man and a woman dressed in the red of operations. They looked familiar, though the lieutenant didn't recall their names. And judging from the hollows beneath their eyes, they were every bit as spooked as he was.

For a moment, Kirk just stood there looking at them, his heart slamming against his ribs so hard it hurt. Then he bent down, hooked his fingers under Ojibwe's armpits, and lifted him again.

"Come on," he told the crewmen, mustering some

authority. "Give me a hand. We've got to get up to the bridge."

At first, they seemed too stunned to acknowledge his command. But after a moment they shrugged off their inertia and surrounded Hasegawa. Between the two of them, they managed to pick him up. Then they carried him out into the corridor and laid him down beside Ojibwe.

Seconds later, they all reentered the lift. Kirk got it moving with another command. As they heard the whine that told them they were traveling through the ship, the lieutenant turned to his companions.

"Where were you?" he asked.

He didn't have to elaborate. They knew exactly what he meant.

"In the forward sensor station," the man told him, "scanning the planet's surface, when that thing attacked us—"

"What was it?" asked the woman.

Kirk turned away from them. "I don't know."

It was the truth—he *didn't* know. But that didn't change anything. It didn't give him anything even approaching an excuse.

A moment later, the three of them arrived at their destination. The lift doors slid open with a mournful gasp, revealing a tableau worse than the lieutenant's worst imaginings.

The *Republic*'s captain, a tall, fair-haired man, was stretched out beside his sleek, metallic center seat. Like the other dead men Kirk had seen on his way to the bridge, Garrovick was bone-white, his cold, dead eyes staring intently at the ceiling.

Commander Tolan, the dark-skinned first officer, sat slumped over his science station, his face hideously illuminated in the lurid red glare of its monitor. Chief Smiley had crumpled at the foot of her engineering console, not far from the sprawled form of Vosberg, the communications officer.

Yu and McKone, the helmsman and the navigator, lay on the deck as well. But their bodies looked composed, as if they had been dragged away from their stations and placed there on purpose—which was, Kirk had no doubt, exactly what had happened.

The only living being in the room was sitting at the helm. Konerko had turned around to face them, her freckled features drawn, her eyes windows on the horror she had to be feeling.

"Lieutenant Kirk," she said, her voice as hollow and lifeless as the bodies around her. "You came."

"Yes," said the lieutenant.

Abandoned consoles beeped softly. Monitors flashed as they displayed one graphic after another. The engines droned.

Nothing had changed. And yet, everything had changed.

Kirk emerged from the turbolift and circumnavigated the captain's chair. Ahead of him, the forward viewscreen displayed a view of space seen from synchronous orbit. The stars wheeled by slowly, almost languidly, easily seen by the naked eye.

Advancing to the helm-navigation console, Kirk sat down beside Konerko and took over the controls. Then he opened an intercom channel.

"This is Lieutenant Kirk," he said, "calling all crewmen. If you can hear me, report your status at the nearest intercom station. Repeat, I need to know your status."

He turned, intending to ask one of the crewmen who had accompanied him in the lift to man the comm station. To the woman's credit, she was already sitting there, monitoring the ship's intercom traffic. The man was making himself useful as well, dragging Vosberg away from the engineering console.

Konerko leaned closer to Kirk. "This couldn't be all of us, could it? I mean, if *we* survived . . ."

"We'll find out soon enough," he told her, watching the acting comm officer and taking comfort in the distraction.

"We're getting some responses," the woman reported. She glanced at the lieutenant. "Lots of them, in fact."

"That's good," said Konerko.

In the next two or three minutes, they received reports from almost every deck on the ship. Some had sustained heavy casualties, some light, and a few had seen no casualties at all. A quick estimate revealed that more than half the crew was still alive.

But that meant almost half the crew was dead.

Kirk swallowed. Half the crew was . . . *more than two hundred people.* His heart sank in his chest. The ship had become a floating morgue, and there was no one left on it who outranked him—no one he could ask for guidance or advice. It was all up to him now.

Konerko was looking at him. They all were, it

seemed—even the staring corpses of the captain and his bridge officers. The engines hummed monotonously, a subtle vibration in the deck below them.

"What do we do now?" someone asked.

"We attend to the dead," the lieutenant decided.

He took a breath, then let it out. Later, there would be time to revile himself. For now, he had a job to do.

Pulling a toggle switch, he opened another intercom channel. "This is Lieutenant Kirk," he began, trying to sound as if he was in command—of himself, at least. "I want you all to listen carefully."

He informed the crew about the fatalities and what he believed had caused them. He told them about the captain and his command staff. Then he assured them all that the danger was over, though he didn't actually know that last part for a fact.

"I'll need parties on every deck to search for bodies," the lieutenant said, "and bring them to the cargo bay. When everyone is accounted for, we'll place a stasis field around them."

To prevent decomposition, Kirk thought. But he didn't say it out loud. The trauma the crew was going through was bad enough without its having to imagine the corpses rotting away.

"Be careful to search everywhere," the lieutenant advised them. "Even in what you think may be the most unlikely places. We've got to make sure to find them all."

In some cases, he knew from experience, it wouldn't require much searching to find the dead; they would be choking the corridors in grotesque, heart-stopping numbers. But in other instances, they might still be lying in their quarters or some obscure part of the ship.

"I'm going to take us to the nearest Starfleet facility," Kirk told them. Consulting his instrument panel, he saw that it would be Starbase 16. "Once we're there, we'll have some time to consider what happened here. In the meantime, I expect you all to discharge your duties to the best of your abilities, just as you did before."

Easier said than done, the lieutenant reflected. But then, it was no more than he was asking of himself.

"Carry on," he finished. "Kirk out."

That done, he turned his attention to his helm controls. In a moment or two, he had made the adjustments necessary to get the ship safely out of the Tycho system. Then he engaged the impulse drive.

There was no response.

The lieutenant checked his monitors. There didn't seem to be any malfunctions in the propulsion assembly—none he could find, anyway. And yet, the ship wasn't moving.

He tried to engage the impulse drive a second time. As before, nothing happened. And whatever the problem was, it wasn't registering on the internal sensor net.

Kirk felt his mouth go dry. This wasn't good, he thought, trying to steady himself. This wasn't good at all.

Without impulse power, their orbit would deteriorate. In fact, he realized with a shock, it had begun to deteriorate already—something Konerko would have noticed if she'd had any experience at navigation. Hell, *he* would have noticed it if he hadn't been focused on taking charge of the ship.

Gleaning the numbers from his monitors, the lieutenant carried out the computation in his head. In nineteen minutes, give or take a few seconds, the ship would start spiraling down toward the planet's surface. A minute and a half after that, the descent would become irreversible.

He was the primary helmsman—maybe the only helmsman left on the ship. He had to do something and he had to do it quickly, before anyone else realized there was something amiss. The crew was on the razor's edge already, Kirk told himself. Something like this, an unexpected danger, might push a few of them over that edge.

Suddenly, the thought came to him . . . could the creature have had something to do with this? Could it have drained the impulse engines as it drained the captain and his command staff?

Probably not, he decided, trying to reason the thing through. It had only attacked living things. There was no evidence it could damage anything else.

"Is something wrong?" asked Konerko.

The lieutenant turned to her. "The impulse drive is offline," he said as calmly as he could.

The ensign's brow puckered with obvious concern. "Offline . . . ? But . . . what's the problem, sir?"

Kirk suppressed a sigh. "I don't know." Then he added, "Yet."

Konerko ran a diagnostic routine. It didn't show anything wrong. *No surprise there*, the lieutenant thought.

He bit his lip, reviewing his options. Unfortunately, he couldn't use the warp drive to leave orbit. The gravity wells of the various planets in the Tycho system would tear the ship apart. It was the first thing they taught you in piloting class.

There was only one alternative. Without hesitation, Kirk slaved his helm controls to the navigation console. Then he got up, came around the captain's chair, and headed for the turbolift.

"Where are you going?" Konerko asked.

"To find out what's wrong," he told her.

"But the helm—" she began.

"—doesn't work," he finished for her, "so it doesn't matter who's sitting there. At ease, Ensign."

A moment later, the turbolift doors opened and he got inside. By then, the lieutenant had already begun picturing the architecture of the impulse drive in his mind.

Certainly, he could have done the same thing at the helm station, and asked one of the other crewman to do the dirty work. But as far as he could tell, none of the survivors possessed his technical know-how.

Besides, Kirk wouldn't have to search the whole ship for the problem—not when he had a clue on which to base his investigation. In fact, he had already isolated it in his mind.

He instructed the turbolift to take him to Deck Seventeen. That was where he would find the only two places on the ship where the impulse relays had been installed within a meter of the internal sensor network.

Certainly, it could have been a coincidence that both the impulse drive and its diagnostic system had failed at the same time. But the lieutenant's instincts told him otherwise. Whatever was responsible for one failure was likely responsible for the other as well.

A moment later, the lift doors parted, revealing Deck Seventeen. There weren't any crewmen in the immediate vicinity, either living or dead. Breathing a sigh of relief, Kirk went over to a panel in the bulkhead, slid it aside and inspected the assortment of tools stored there.

Selecting two of them as well as a tricorder, he closed the panel and continued on his way. He made two left turns before the corridor led him to a duranium ladder—and the kind of hatch door that gave entry to the ship's ubiquitous Jefferies tubes.

Climbing the ladder and swinging the door open, the lieutenant clambered up into the tube. It was a long, cramped cylinder full of conduits and flashing circuitry that connected with other cylinders full of conduits and circuitry—all of it designed to provide access to the vessel's various systems, propulsion and internal sensors included.

The sound of the engines was stronger here, unshielded. It drummed in his head like a giant heartbeat.

Some thirty meters up ahead, there was a junction. Kirk turned left there and kept crawling. Another twenty meters up, he came to the place where he suspected the problem might be.

Activating his tricorder, he scanned the area. But everything seemed to be working there—both the propulsion relays and the sensor net. He gazed back down the tube. He would have to retrace his steps to find the other possible trouble site.

Doggedly, the lieutenant crawled back the way he had come. After a few minutes, he passed the hatch through which he had entered the tube in the first place. Then he kept going in the other direction, turned at the first junction, and came in sight of his destination.

He had expected to see an empty Jefferies tube, just like the others. What he discovered was something else entirely.

There was a human being lying there amid the flashing lights, sprawled faceup across the curvature of the tube. What's more, Kirk recognized him. His name was Lieutenant Crane. He had worked in engineering.

The lieutenant swallowed. The thing had been here as well, he thought, a chill climbing the rungs of his spine. It had gotten into the Jefferies tubes as well as the corridors and the bridge. In fact, for all he knew, it might still be there.

Just beyond the next junction, it occurred to him. Or maybe the one directly behind him . . .

Kirk whirled, thinking he had glimpsed something white and gaseous out of the corner of his eye. But there wasn't anything there—just another narrow cylinder full of data conduits and relay circuits.

Taking a breath to steady himself, he turned around again and advanced to the spot where Crane was stretched out. It didn't take the lieutenant more than a moment to see that the man was dead, his face every bit as pale and icy cold-looking as Piniella's or Gilhooley's.

There was something clutched in the engineer's hand. Looking closer, Kirk saw that it was a tricorder, just like the one he had brought with him. Apparently, someone had noticed the impulse problem earlier, traced its origin to this location, and dispatched Crane to take care of it. But before he could do anything, he had been killed.

Like all the rest, the lieutenant thought. Like the two hundred others who had been turned into porcelain statues.

Clenching his jaw, Kirk got to work. First, he used his tricorder to identify the problem—a breakdown in one of the relays that provided power to the driver coil assembly. Then he used his spanner to bypass the problem and render the system intact again.

A simple correction, really. Ridiculously simple. But without it, the ship's impulse drive would have remained useless to them.

The repair complete, the lieutenant gathered up his tools and made his way back toward the hatch. He still had a few minutes left, he judged, to contact Konerko via the intercom and have her engage the drive.

It would not be very difficult. After all, he had already charted a course. All she would have to do was implement it.

Unfortunately, there was no time for Kirk to drag Crane out of the tube—not when their orbit was deteriorating more and more with each breath he took. But he would be sure to have someone go in and get the man.

The lieutenant owed Crane that much, at least.

Chapter Five

LIEUTENANT JUNIOR GRADE Gary Mitchell stood in the lounge of the *U.S.S. Constitution* along with the ship's command staff, surrounded by off-duty crewmen playing three-dimensional chess, drinking from mugs and swapping jokes.

Despite the laughter he heard, the lieutenant was the happiest man in the room—as happy, in fact, as a sloppy, fat Orion with a belly full of warm, juicy wing-slugs. But then, there was a reason for his good mood. He was going to see his old friend again.

Mitchell had never doubted that Jim Kirk would do well for himself. He had always known the man would rise through the ranks of the Fleet faster than a shooting star, eclipsing his peers along the way.

After all, Kirk had been earmarked years ago as a guy with exemplary command potential. He had been the darling of Starfleet Command almost since the day he set foot on the grounds of the Academy.

Of course, the path of Mitchell's own career had never been anywhere that assured. Since day one, he had slacked off in his studies at the Academy, repeatedly disobeyed the orders of his superiors, defied the customs of alien cultures, and generally made a nuisance of himself. In a way, it was a miracle he had gotten anywhere.

Fortunately for Mitchell, Kirk and others had seen some potential in him. They had stood up for him and defended his actions whenever he went out too far on a limb. And through their grace, he had earned himself a berth on one of the Fleet's premiere starships six months earlier.

So when Mitchell had learned that his friend would be serving on the same vessel with him, the amazing part wasn't that they would be plying the stars together again, just as they did at the Academy. The amazing part was that Mitchell was plying the stars at all.

Feeling a hand on his shoulder, he turned and found himself looking into the face of the *Constitution*'s first officer. "Your friend is late," said Commander Hirota, affecting an expression of disapproval beneath his brush of jet black hair.

Mitchell shook his head with the utmost confidence. "There must be a problem with the transporter on the base. Jim Kirk's never been late for anything in his life."

"You know," said Chief Engineer Jankowski, a dirty blonde with sensuous lips and an infectious smile, "you're not making it easy on your friend, Lieutenant. After hearing so much about him, we'll all be disappointed if he doesn't walk on water."

"On a starship," Hirota pointed out, "that would be difficult to prove one way or the other."

"I'll tell you from experience," Mitchell told them, "he doesn't walk on water. But believe me, that's the *only* thing about him that'll disappoint you. You know what *I'm* like, right?"

"Right," said Jankowski.

"Well," said Mitchell, "Kirk's even better."

"So's a Denebian slime devil," remarked Lynch, a dark-skinned man with chiseled features who served as the ship's science officer. Technically, he was also Mitchell's superior, since navigation fell under the jurisdiction of the science section. "On the other hand," the man continued, "we're not bringing a slime devil aboard as our primary helmsman."

That got a laugh from Hirota and Jankowski—not to mention a chortle from Borrik, the bowlegged communications officer with the long face and the zebralike markings on his skin. Mitchell felt compelled to give as good as he got, the product of growing up on the streets of New York.

"A Denebian slime devil," he told Lynch, "wouldn't have the guts to work the helm. He'd be more suited to . . . oh, say, the science station."

That got an even bigger laugh. Lynch's eyes narrowed as he approached Mitchell and went nose to nose with him, making a point with his imposing height. But the younger man stood his ground.

"I'd kill you for that," said the science officer, "if

you weren't so damned entertaining to have around."
Then he clapped Mitchell on the shoulder and
laughed as heartily as anybody else.

"I'm glad everyone's having such a good time," said
a familiar voice—one that resounded with authority.

Suddenly, the room fell silent. Mitchell turned
along with everyone else and saw the robust form of
Captain Augenthaler fill the entrance to the lounge,
his small, blue eyes screwed up in mock disapproval.

The captain wasn't alone, either. There was an
athletic-looking fellow standing alongside him, a
young man with neatly combed, golden brown hair
and a face that spoke of cornfields and wide-open
skies.

"Sorry, sir," Hirota responded, straightfaced. "We
didn't mean to have a good time in your absence."

There were smiles all around. Mitchell smiled as
well, certain that Augenthaler would take the first
officer's remark in the spirit in which it had been
tendered.

"Apology accepted," said the captain. He made a
gesture to include everyone in the room. "As you
were, people."

The room began to buzz again, though not quite as
loudly as before. After all, nearly everyone present
wanted to know what Augenthaler was up to.

The captian took in his command staff with a
glance. "If you can all stop chuckling for a moment,
I'd like you to meet our new lieutenant . . . Jim
Kirk."

Mitchell grinned. It was good to see the old cur-
mudgeon again. In fact, it was damned good. And

wasn't it just typical of Kirk to look like he'd lost his best pal when everyone around him was in such a good mood?

As long as Mitchell had known him, Kirk had always been a bit too serious for his own good. And every time it seemed the man had loosened up a little, he did something to demonstrate conclusively that he was still the same stick-in-the-mud as always.

Mitchell's impulse was to wrap an arm around Kirk's shoulders and present the lieutenant to the command staff. However, that job belonged to Captain Augenthaler, and the last thing a junior officer wanted to do was step on his commanding officer's toes.

"Lieutenant Kirk," said the captain, "allow me to introduce my staff. My first officer, Commander Akira Hirota."

Hirota inclined his head. "Welcome to the *Constitution,* Lieutenant. I look forward to working with you."

"Likewise, sir," Kirk replied.

Augenthaler went on. "And this," he said with a sweep of his arm, "is Christina Velasquez, my chief medical officer."

The doctor was a slight woman with long, dark hair and light blue eyes, who had remained on the periphery of the conversation until that moment. She smiled warmly at the newcomer. "I've heard a lot about you, Mr. Kirk. Mr. Mitchell has seen to that."

Kirk acknowledged the CMO's comment with a nod. "I'm pleased to meet you too, Doctor."

Next, the captain identified Lieutenant Lynch, the

science officer, and Chief Gaynor, who was in charge of security on the ship. Gaynor was a barrel-chested, powerful-looking man. Like Velasquez, he had remained relatively aloof to that point.

"Good to make your acquaintance," said Lynch.

"Same here," Gaynor muttered.

Kirk responded as Mitchell would have expected— politely and economically—but he seemed unusually reserved, even for a stick-in-the-mud. *Maybe the guy's a little nervous,* Mitchell told himself. *Yeah, that's it. After all, this is his first assignment as second officer of a starship, and he wants to make the most of it.*

"This," said Augenthaler, making his way around the room, "is Anita Jankowski, the *Consitution*'s chief engineer. And beside her is Mr. Borrik, our communications officer."

Borrik was a Dedderac, one of the first aliens Mitchell had ever served alongside. In keeping with his people's traditions, he inclined his long, striped head and held his slender hands out, palms up—an offer of friendship and peace.

Jankowski was less formal. "Nice to have you aboard," she said.

"Nice to be aboard," Kirk told her. But there was no real animation in his voice. He seemed cool almost to the point of disinterest.

The captain must not have noticed, because he went on with his introductions. "Finally," he said, "someone I believe you know." He indicated Mitchell with a jerk of his thumb. "Our navigator, God help us."

Kirk turned to him and their eyes met. But even

then, seeing the pal he hadn't spoken to in months, there wasn't any real life in him. It was as if the lieutenant hardly knew him.

Strange, Mitchell thought.

"Fancy meeting you here," he said.

"Fancy that," Kirk responded.

But there was none of the old warmth in his voice, none of the old camaraderie. At that point, Mitchell had to wonder if Kirk's problem was more than mere nervousness.

Augenthaler put his hand on Kirk's shoulder. "Of course, you'll be spending most of your time at the helm, Lieutenant. And when you're there, Mr. Mitchell will be paired with you as navigator."

Kirk nodded. "Thank you," he told the captain.

"Don't mention it," said Augenthaler. "Just do the job I know you're capable of, Mr. Kirk, and that'll be thanks enough."

A moment later, the captain dismissed everyone and sent them about their business. As it happened, Mitchell and his friend were the last to remain standing in the lounge.

By then, the crewmen seated around them seemed to have lost interest in Augenthaler's meeting. They were playing chess, filling their mugs and exchanging jokes again.

Kirk glanced at Mitchell, but he didn't say anything. He just stood there with a funny, blank look in his eyes. The junior officer wasn't sure why his friend looked so distant, so disoriented, but he was determined to bring him out of it.

"How do you like that?" he asked, grinning.

"Mitchell and Kirk, back in business again and more black-hearted than ever. If I were Starfleet, I'd be putting out warning beacons all over the sector."

His friend looked at him. "That's funny," he said, but without a whole lot of conviction.

Mitchell returned the look. "You okay, Jim?"

Kirk didn't answer him. He just looked away.

When the man spoke again, it was about something else entirely. "By the way," he said, "thanks for putting in a good word for me here. On the *Constitution,* I mean."

Mitchell shrugged. "No problem whatsoever. For some reason, the captain seems to respect my opinion in such matters . . . even if I voice it more frequently than he'd like."

Kirk smiled, but it was a shadow of what it should have been. What it had been, back at the Academy.

"Besides," Mitchell added slyly, "you weren't very hard to sell. I mean, the hero of the *Farragut?* Augenthaler couldn't wait to get his captainly hands on you."

His friend nodded, but his mind seemed light-years away. "Hero of the *Farragut.* That's a good one," he said.

Funny, Mitchell thought. Kirk sounded almost bitter about what he had done on the *Farragut.* But as far as anyone had heard—and admittedly, it wasn't very much, since Starfleet Command had kept it tightly under wraps—his friend had exhibited great courage and presence of mind. According to one rumor, he had saved the lives of the entire crew.

But maybe he hadn't saved everyone, the navigator

realized, experiencing one of his special flashes of insight. Maybe a few of Kirk's friends on the *Farragut* had gotten hurt or died. And maybe he was worrying about them, or even mourning their loss.

Yeah, Mitchell told himself. *That would explain the way the man's acting. Hell, I'd be acting that way too, under the circumstances.*

"Jim," he said, "something happened on the *Farragut,* didn't it? Something that's got you down?"

Kirk's eyes seemed to recede into his skull. "I think I'm going to like it here," he said, changing the subject. It came out mechanically, as if he'd practiced saying it in front of a mirror.

Damn, Mitchell thought. *It's worse than him acting like he doesn't know me. It's like he's not even here.*

He felt a desperate need to fan a spark in his friend, to make it seem like old times. For a second or two, he plumbed his memory for something optimistic, something upbeat.

"Hey," he said finally, "I heard Finney forgave you."

Ben Finney had been Kirk's friend at the Academy until an unfortunate incident came between them. One night on a training flight, Kirk had relieved Finney on watch and found an open circuit that could have blown up the ship. Kirk closed the circuit and logged the incident, earning Finney a reprimand . . . and last place on the all-important promotion list.

Afterward, Finney had felt betrayed. After all, Kirk was his pal—he could have overlooked the incident. But when it came to the safety of the crew, Kirk went strictly by the book, no exceptions.

Mitchell hadn't always liked that about him. But at the moment, he would've settled even for that Kirk. Anything was better than the one standing in front of him.

"Is it true?" Mitchell asked.

Kirk sighed. "Yes," he said softly. "We're friends again."

He didn't sound very happy about it—and yet, Kirk's guilt about the incident had haunted him for a long time. If Finney had let him off the hook, Kirk should have been ecstatic.

Mitchell's lips pressed together. This wasn't good, he told himself. This wasn't good at all.

He had looked forward to picking up where he and Kirk had left off. He had looked forward to their being a team again. But his friend seemed so melancholy, so faraway . . . and maybe something else as well, though Mitchell couldn't put his finger on it despite his powers of intuition.

Someone started playing some music on an alien flute. It was light, upbeat, optimistic . . . and grotesquely inappropriate, given the tone of the officers' conversation.

"I guess I'll show you to your quarters," Mitchell said, feeling that he had lost a battle of some kind.

Kirk nodded. "That'd be great."

Yeah, the junior officer thought. *Great.* "Come on," he told his friend. "They're on Deck Four, right near mine."

And he led the way.

Chapter Six

As Kirk walked the long, straight corridor that led to the rec lounge, he kept his eyes straight ahead and tried not to think about what he might find if he looked at the floor.

After all, the *Constitution* and the *Farragut* were sister ships. Everything about the vessels was identical except for the commissioning plaques on their bridges. Given all those similarities, it was difficult for the second officer to keep from glancing at the deck here and there and seeing the faces of his dead comrades staring up at him.

Pavano, Gilhooley, Keyes, Poquette . . . all of them blue-lipped and pale as ivory, all of them drained of their life's blood through an invisible wound, all of them caught at their moment of greatest terror.

It's all right, Kirk told himself, managing to stay

calm. *They're not here. You left them all behind on the* Farragut, *remember?*

Of course, the lieutenant had never truly believed otherwise, even at the worst of times. He had never gone insane enough to think his friends' corpses were following him from place to place, crying out for retribution. Nonetheless, their likenesses were emblazoned on Kirk's brain, branded there like ghostly afterimages, and he was afraid it would be a long time before those images faded.

Turning a corner, the lieutenant saw the double doors of the rec lounge up ahead. They parted well before he got there, letting out two of his crewmates. Kirk didn't look them in the eye. He just continued walking, the doors remaining open for him until he got past them.

Only then did he look around. There were a good twenty or twenty-five people in the lounge, but Gary wasn't one of them. The second officer sighed. His friend was late and he was hungry—and knowing Gary, there was no telling when he might show up.

Another time, years earlier, he might have gotten mad at Gary. He might have had words with him about his paying more attention to the time. But not anymore. Now, Kirk couldn't have cared less.

He decided to get some food and sit down somewhere. If his friend arrived any time in the next half hour or so, he could join him. If not, he would see Gary another time.

Picking up a tray from a stack at one end of the counter, the lieutenant slid it along until he got to the food slot. There, with a series of beeps, he punched in his meager requirements—a tuna casserole and a cup of black coffee.

Not that it mattered much what he ordered. Nothing seemed very good to him these days. It was as if his taste buds had died along with Captain Garrovick and the others on the *Farragut.*

Garrovick, he thought, as he picked up his tray and turned around. It still hurt to recall the man. Garrovick had liked him, treated him almost like a son. And how had he—

"What the hell!" someone cried.

Before Kirk knew it, he had come nose to nose with the person. The second officer's tray, wedged between them, flipped forward and deposited its contents on the other man's uniform.

It took him a moment to realize the other man was Jack Gaynor.

The security chief's mouth twisted in anger, and he started to reach for the front of Kirk's shirt. Then he seemed to remember he was dealing with a superior officer. Red-faced, the muscles in his jaw rippling, Gaynor took a breath and let it out.

"Sorry, sir," he muttered. "Clumsy of me."

Aware that everyone in the room was staring at him, the second officer shook his head. "No, Chief, it was my fault. I wasn't watching where I was—"

But before he could say anything more, Gaynor held his hand up. "Don't," he snarled almost menacingly, his shirtfront wet and stained and giving off wisps of steam. And then, in an only slightly less antagonistic tone, "Just don't, all right?"

Then he turned and flipped Kirk's empty tray at the

refuse aperture. The thing missed and clattered to the floor, but Gaynor didn't bother to pick it up. He just headed for the doors.

A voice rang out. "Just a minute, mister!"

As the echoes died, the security chief stopped in his tracks and turned around. Hirota was bearing down on him like a photon torpedo, his expression vastly different from that of the friendly, easygoing man who had welcomed the second officer aboard the ship.

"Sir?" said Gaynor, glancing not at the first officer but at Kirk. His eyes were full of anger and resentment.

"If I were you," Hirota told him in a clipped voice, "I'd apologize to Lieutenant Kirk. Then I'd pick up that tray and be grateful I wasn't tossed in the brig for acting like a child."

Gaynor stared at Hirota for a moment, then turned to the second officer. "I hope you'll excuse my behavior, sir," he said. But his tone still had an arrogance about it.

As Kirk and the first officer and everyone else in the rec lounge watched, the security chief knelt and picked up the errant tray and placed it in the proper slot. Then, without another word, he made his exit.

The second officer shook his head. The whole thing had been his fault, just as he said. He had been thinking about the people on the *Farragut* and Gaynor had paid the price for it.

If he couldn't maneuver around the rec lounge, Kirk thought, what good was he going to be at the helm of a starship? What good was he going to be as a second officer?

The brief moment of excitement over and done with, a buzz of conversation began to fill the room again. Little by little, the place was returning to normal.

Bending down, Kirk recovered his plasticware, his casserole dish and his coffee cup. As he got to his feet, he found himself surrounded by Lynch, Velasquez, and Jankowski. Still holding the casserole dish and the empty coffee cup in his hands, he looked around at the three of them and wondered what they wanted from him.

"Pay no attention to Chief Gaynor," said the science officer. "He's always been a hothead."

"Lynch is right," Velasquez agreed. "He can't accept the fact that he was passed over for second officer."

"Second officer?" Kirk echoed.

"A little while before you got the job," Jankowski explained. "I think you get the picture."

The helmsman nodded. "I think so, yes."

It was pretty obvious. Gaynor was a career officer, and Kirk was a man several years his junior—an upstart, in the security chief's eyes. It was no wonder the man harbored some resentment.

"Anyway," Jankowski went on, "I don't see what all the fuss is about." She glanced at Hirota, who was standing across the room. "It's not like our first officer is ever going to need replacing."

Hirota must have overheard, because he looked back at her. The engineer smiled at him. Clearly, Kirk thought, there was a bond between them that went beyond mere camaraderie.

"Thanks for your support," the second officer told his fellow officers. "But, really, I don't need it. I'm fine."

They regarded him. "You're sure?" asked Lynch.

"I'm sure," Kirk replied.

Dumping the remains of his first lunch in the appropriate aperture, he went and got another one. Then he found a seat at an empty table, where the friendly chatter wasn't quite so loud. As he put his tray down, he saw that Lynch, Velasquez, and Jankowski were still standing where he had left them, watching him. Finally, they returned to their places on the other side of the room, and he began to eat his food.

No doubt his colleagues were wondering about his solitary behavior, trying to divine if it was Gaynor's outburst that had caused it. Of course, Gaynor had nothing to do with it. Kirk just didn't want to be in a position where he would have to make small talk with strangers.

It was hard enough for the second officer to maintain his composure if he just fixed his gaze on his tray. If he looked around too much, he might begin to remember what it had been like in the *Farragut*'s rec lounge before the disaster, and he wanted to avoid that at all costs.

He had believed that it would help him to sign on with the *Constitution*—to leap back into the fray with both feet. Wasn't that what he'd always been told? If you're afraid of something, confront it. Go nose to nose with it. Show your fear who's boss.

But now, Kirk was starting to wonder if coming

here had been such a good idea after all. The last thing he wanted was to crack under the strain and become useless to his fellow crewmen.

Abruptly, he realized his casserole dish was empty. Likewise, his coffee cup, except for a thin film on the bottom. Getting up, the second officer brought his tray to the refuse slot and emptied it. Then he crossed the room and left the mess hall, its voices dying behind him.

He hadn't gone far, however, before he heard another sound—that of approaching footsteps. Turning to glance over his shoulder, he saw that Borrik was coming after him.

The communications officer wasn't the first Dedderac Kirk had ever met. After all, there were a couple dozen of them scattered throughout the Fleet on one ship or another.

Generally, the second officer had found, Dedderacs were a thoughtful, quiet, and efficient breed who performed extremely well under pressure. Judging from the way he carried himself, Borrik was no exception.

"Lieutenant Kirk," said the communications officer, "stop, please. I wish to speak with you for a moment."

The human did as he was asked. "What about?"

"About Lieutenant Gaynor," said Borrik. His nostrils flared. "He can be something of an idiot sometimes."

Kirk found it hard to disagree.

"However," the Dedderac continued, "he is not as big an idiot as he appeared a few minutes ago."

"Oh?" Kirk responded.

"Jack Gaynor is a proud man. A professional. He has been aiming for the second officer's post for a long time."

"Is that so."

Borrik regarded him with his pale yellow eyes. "No doubt," he said, "it is difficult for a young man to understand what Lieutenant Gaynor is feeling . . . what it is like to be passed over for a promotion. But someday, you may find yourself in a similar position."

Kirk nodded. "You want me to excuse the way he acted."

The Dedderac shook his striped head. "I only want you to understand where his behavior came from."

The second officer sighed. "You don't have to make any excuses for Gaynor," he said. "I don't bear him any ill will."

Borrik's eyes narrowed. "Really?"

"Really," Kirk confirmed. "Now, if you'll excuse me . . ."

The Dedderac nodded. "Of course."

With a faint, sad smile, the younger man headed for the nearest turbolift, leaving the incident behind him. With all the nightmarish things he had on his mind, Gaynor's fit simply hadn't fazed him very much.

But then, these days, few things did.

Damn, thought Mitchell, rushing along the corridor so quickly it might have been easier for him to break into a run. Of all the times for his chronometer to go on the blink.

His friend Jim would be angry with him. He was

sure of it. The man hated to be kept waiting more than anything, and Mitchell had been guilty of it so many times he had no credibility left.

If this had happened at some other time and in some other place, the navigator wouldn't have felt quite so bad about it. But Jim had been acting so strangely since he came on board, Mitchell had really wanted to shepherd him through whatever he was going through.

It's difficult to do that when you can't even show up on time for lunch, he told himself. *Damn that chronometer!*

In his haste, the junior officer passed several crewmen going in the other direction and then overtook a few others. They all stared at him, no doubt wondering why he was in such a hurry.

Finally, he spun around a corner and got the rec lounge in his sights. He pelted down the last stretch of hallway and then slowed down just before he hit the double set of red doors. Taking a deep breath, he waited for them to open for him.

A moment later, they whispered apart, revealing the lounge and everything in it. The place was pretty crowded, Mitchell thought, even for lunchtime. However, it didn't take him more than a quick look to determine that his friend wasn't there.

Seeing Lynch, Velasquez, and Jankowski sitting together, the navigator went over to their table. "You didn't, by any chance, see Jim Kirk here?" he asked his fellow officers.

"As a matter of fact," said the chief engineer, "we did. He left just a couple of moments ago."

Mitchell frowned. "Thanks." He started for the exit.

"Gary!" Lynch called out.

The navigator turned. "Yes?"

"There was a little trouble," the science officer told him.

Concerned, Mitchell found himself sitting down with the others. "What kind of trouble? Is Jim all right?"

"He's fine," said Velasquez. "All that happened is he spilled his meal on Jack Gaynor. It was an accident, of course. But under the circumstances, Jack took it personally."

"Circumstances?" the navigator echoed.

Lynch turned to the doctor. "He doesn't know."

Mitchell looked at the science officer. "Know what?"

That was when Velasquez told him about Gaynor's aspiration to become the *Constitution*'s second officer—an aspiration thwarted by Kirk's appointment to the post. Suddenly, the navigator understood.

"Gaynor resents Jim," he said. "So when Jim spilled his food on Gaynor, the guy blew up."

"Something like that," Jankowski confirmed.

"Jack tossed his tray at the refuse slot and started to stalk out of here," Lynch related. "And if our erstwhile First Officer Hirota hadn't taken him to task, that's the way it would have ended. As it was, Jack apologized and put the tray where it belonged."

Mitchell grunted. "And what did Jim do?"

The officers looked at one another. Jankowski shrugged.

"Not much of anything, really," she replied. "He just stood there. When Jack was gone and Kirk was picking up his dishes, we went over to him—tried to explain why Jack acted the way he did."

"Just the way we explained it to you," Lynch added.

"And how did he react?" the navigator asked.

Again, his colleagues exchanged glances. "He still pretty much just stood there," the science officer told him. "Then he got some more food and went off to eat by himself."

Just the way he used to at the Academy, Mitchell thought. But in those days, it hadn't been Kirk's choice to remain apart from society—it was just the way things had worked out.

"Is . . . Kirk all right?" Jankowski wondered.

The navigator turned to Velasquez. "I believe that's a question for the chief medical officer here."

Velasquez smiled. "You know I can't discuss the man's medical records. But if you're asking me as a friend and not a doctor, I'd say he's got something on his mind."

"That's how it seems to me, too," Mitchell noted.

Lynch regarded him. "Did you ask Kirk about it?"

The navigator nodded. "He didn't exactly seem eager to comment, but I think it has something to do with the *Farragut*. I mean, he got a commendation and all, but I wonder if some of his friends got hurt in the course of whatever happened—or maybe even died."

"Is that one of your patented flashes of insight?" Jankowski asked.

Mitchell looked at her. "Could be. I just wish the

flash were a little brighter so I could figure out my pal's problem."

No one said anything after that. Sighing, the navigator got up and pulled down on the front of his uniform.

"I guess I ought to look in on him. I have an apology to make for showing up late," he said.

As his comrades wished him luck, Mitchell left the buzz of the rec lounge and headed for the nearest turbolift. He felt sorry for his friend. He plumbed his imagination for a way to cheer the man up—a way to take his mind off whatever was bothering him.

By the time the lift doors hissed apart for him, he had an idea. What's more, it was one he had used with success in the past. Unfortunately, when he reached Deck Four and the doors opened again, he hadn't come up with anything else to use as a backup.

The navigator's door was the fifth one on the right. Jim's was two doors before it, on the same side of the corridor. Mitchell stopped there and gave the internal sensor a chance to register his presence.

Before too long, the door slid away, revealing the interior of his friend's quarters. Jim was standing in the middle of a surprisingly bare-walled anteroom, looking weary and put upon. He didn't at all seem like the man with whom the navigator had gone through the Academy.

"You were late," said the second officer, but the remark didn't have the fire of an accusation. It was just a statement of fact.

"I was," Mitchell conceded. "Sorry about that."

Kirk looked at him a moment longer, as if he were

going to say something else. Then he just turned and retreated to his workstation, where it appeared he had been working on something.

The navigator came around behind his friend to find out what was on the monitor screen. He wasn't surprised to see a three-dimensional-chess program in operation. After all, the game had become Kirk's passion by the time he graduated the Academy, even more so than racquetball or gymnastics.

At that particular juncture, only a couple of moves had been made. Mitchell smiled. "I'd give you some advice," he told his friend, "but I doubt I could suggest anything you hadn't already thought of."

The second officer didn't answer. He just tapped in another move and watched as it was reflected on the monitor screen.

"You know," the navigator ventured, "Mr. Borrik is pretty good at this. I bet he'd give you a run for your money."

Still no answer. Kirk just continued to stare at the chess pieces arrayed on the screen.

"What do you say?" Mitchell asked. "Should I see if he's got time for a game later on?"

Finally, his friend spared him a glance. "No, thanks," he answered softly. "I'm content to try my luck against the computer." Then he turned back to his virtual chess game.

The navigator sighed. So much for that approach. But he still had the ammunition with which he had armed himself in the turbolift.

"Listen," he said, "I happened to run into Ensign Lidell last night. You know who I mean? The slender redhead with the amazing green eyes and the legs that go forever? Anyway, I bet she'd love to tour the botanical garden with the *Constitution*'s dashing new second officer."

Kirk shook his head. "Maybe another time."

"But, Jim," Mitchell protested, kneeling down next to his friend to get the man's attention, "I didn't mention a time."

The second officer looked at him. "I appreciate what you're doing," he said, "trying to make me feel at home here and all. But really, I'm fine the way I am. All right?"

There wasn't a whole lot the navigator could say to that. "Sure," he managed. "Whatever you say."

Kirk nodded. "Thanks."

Then he went back to his chess program.

Gary stared at him. There had to be a way to snap his friend out of his malaise, he told himself. But at the moment, he didn't have any idea what that way might be.

Chapter Seven

KIRK HAD BEEN sitting behind the *Constitution*'s sleek, black helm controls for a good half hour, running diagnostic after red-screened diagnostic to keep his nightmares at bay, when he heard a beep. Glancing over his shoulder, he saw Lieutenant Borrik swivel himself away from his communication panel.

"Captain?" said the Dedderac, an undertone of urgency in his voice.

Captain Augenthaler, who had been going over inventory reports with Yeoman Ferris, turned in his chair to face Borrik. So did Kirk and everyone else on the bridge—his friend Gary, Science Officer Lynch, Chief Engineer Jankowski, and Commander Hirota.

"Yes, Lieutenant?" the captain responded.

"Sir," said the communications officer, "I have a

message for you from Starfleet Command . . . for your eyes only."

"Is that so?" said Augenthaler. Rising from his center seat, he glanced at his yeoman. "We'll continue this later," he told her.

"Aye, sir," Ferris responded.

"Commander Hirota," said the captain as he moved to the turbolift, "you have the conn. I'll be in the briefing room."

Finishing his work at one of the peripheral stations, the first officer nodded. "Acknowledged, sir."

Then the lift doors opened for Augenthaler and he entered the compartment. The doors had barely closed again before Kirk saw the bridge officers exchanging curious glances.

"The captain's eyes only," Jankowski noted from her place at the engineering console, just to one side of the lift doors. "Sounds ominous."

"Maybe it's the Klingons again," Lynch ventured, caught in the crimson glare of his science station monitors.

"It's always the Klingons," the engineer shot back at him.

"Maybe it's war this time," said the science officer, a devilish expression spreading across his face.

"Bite your tongue," Hirota told him, getting up and crossing to the captain's chair. "The last thing we need now is another Donatu Five."

"I thought we won that battle," Gary said.

"We did," the first officer replied, "but not before both sides suffered heavy casualties." He turned to

Lynch. "I'd keep that in mind before I tempted fate with any clever remarks."

"Sorry, sir," said the science officer, though it was clear his apology was only half-serious.

Kirk could tell from their banter that these people liked each other. Part of him wanted to be liked by them as well. But then, he had felt that way about Captain Garrovick and his staff, and it had made it all the more painful when the life was sucked out of them.

He would maintain his distance from this crew, the second officer promised himself. He would keep them at arm's length—all of them, including his friend Gary. After all, he had all the ghosts he could handle.

Just as he thought that, the turbolift door opened again with a rush of air, and Captain Augenthaler walked out. His expression was a pensive one as he returned to his seat and sat down.

No one asked a question of him, but it was in the air nonetheless. What's more, Augenthaler seemed to know it.

"We've received new orders," he said.

New orders, Kirk thought. There was a time when those words would have stirred his sense of adventure. No longer, though. Now he was just trying to cope, just trying to maintain his sanity.

"Mr. Kirk," said the captain.

The helmsman turned in his chair. "Yes, sir?"

"Bring us about, heading two seven eight mark four," Augenthaler told him crisply, his small blue eyes looking more intense than usual. "And while you're at it, Lieutenant, increase speed to warp six."

"Aye, sir," Kirk replied, implementing the changes in course and velocity through his helm controls. A series of short, shrill sounds punctuated his actions.

Hirota moved to the side of the captain's chair. "I don't suppose you'd care to let us in on where we're going, sir."

"Unfortunately," said Augenthaler, "I can't do that, Commander. And not because it's classified." His frown deepened. "It's because I don't know myself. We've been asked by Command to proceed on this course until we receive further instructions. Period, end of transmission."

The first officer absorbed the information. "Well, then," he declared, "I guess that's what we'll do."

The captain stroked his rounded chin. "On the other hand," he said thoughtfully, "there's nothing to keep us from gathering as much information as we can." He glanced at Gary. "Is there, Lieutenant Mitchell?"

"No, sir," said the junior officer. His fingers were already flying over his navigational controls, the red and green graphics on his monitor screens changing rapidly. "No reason at all."

Clearly, Kirk mused, Augenthaler trusted his bridge crew implictly. Otherwise, the captain would never have asked his people to investigate what Starfleet obviously wanted kept under wraps.

"Anything, Mr. Mitchell?" Augenthaler wondered out loud.

Gary was studying one of his secondary navigation monitors, where he had called up a three-dimensional coordinate matrix. "Nothing much, sir," he replied after a moment or two. "Ultimately, of course, we're headed for the heart of the Klingon Neutral Zone, but there doesn't seem to be anything of real significance between here and there—just a single star system with three unoccupied planets."

Then the navigator's brow furrowed—as if he had noticed something unusual after all. But he didn't say anything more.

Unable to see Gary's face, the captain grunted and leaned back in his chair. "There must be something, Mr. Mitchell—even if it's a situation only Starfleet has any knowledge of."

But Gary seemed to have some knowledge of it, too. The more Kirk stared at his friend, the more he studied Gary's expression, the more certain he was that Gary knew something.

Intrigued, the helmsman decided to figure out why. Calling up a blood-red coordinate matrix of his own, he scanned it to see what systems or starbases might lie near their new course. But as Gary had indicated, there wasn't anything noteworthy in their path. Just that lone star and its planets, a handful of light-years from the Klingon Neutral Zone.

Strange, Kirk thought. He could have sworn that his friend had discovered something interesting.

Then, as if the navigator had heard the helmsman's question, he turned and regarded him. Slowly and unobtrusively, Gary's finger moved in a circle around a particular part of his secondary monitor screen—encompassing a handful of the hundreds of emerald-green coordinates in the matrix he had created.

At first, Kirk didn't understand what his friend was trying to say. What was it about that portion of the matrix that he was supposed to recognize? What meaning was it supposed to have for him?

Then it hit him.

My god, he thought. It was the same part of space he and Gary had visited all those years ago . . . a place where they had been part of something dark and mysterious, though neither he nor his friend had ever learned what that something might be.

Now they were going back to that part of the void, a sector seldom visited by Federation ships or anyone else. If luck was with them, Kirk mused, they would get an opportunity to plumb the mystery again—and maybe this time get to the bottom of it.

He raised his eyes and met Gary's look. *I get it,* he answered silently. What's more, he had figured out why his friend couldn't let the captain in on his conjecture.

After all, they had sworn never to talk about it. Not with anyone—their commanding officers included. And despite Gary's casual ways, he had always been a man of his word.

From the moment Mitchell had realized where the *Constitution* might be headed, he had been itching to talk to Kirk about it. But as long as he was at the navigation console, he couldn't do that.

So he waited patiently for his shift to end, enduring each moment as if it were an hour and each hour as if it were a week. Finally, the time began to approach when the navigator could turn his responsibilities over to another crewman and share his excitement with his friend.

Then, when Mitchell was less than half an hour from the end of his shift, he heard a beep from Borrik's communications console. Out of the corner of his eye, he saw the Dedderac stir and say, "I have another call for you, Captain. Eyes only, as before."

Augenthaler looked back over his shoulder. "From Starfleet Command again?" he inquired.

Borrik shook his striped head from side to side. "No, sir. This time it's from Starbase Twenty-nine. An Admiral Mangione."

Mitchell felt a thrill go up and down his spine. He'd been right about their heading, hadn't he? And Mangione's involvement in the mission was proof of it.

Seven years earlier, he and Kirk had been cadets on the starship *Republic,* dispatched on a routine training mission not far from the Klingon border. Rollin Bannock had been the captain on that voyage . . . and Ellen Mangione had been the first officer.

For a while, everything had gone according to plan. Then, one night as they skirted the Klingon neutral zone, Mangione had gotten on the intercom system and ordered all cadets to confine themselves to their quarters. Naturally, Kirk did as the first officer told him. So did Mitchell, albeit a good deal more reluctantly.

But afterward, his curiosity had nearly eaten him alive. And when the cadets' confinement was over, and it was clear their captain had no intention of telling them what had transpired, Mitchell hadn't been able to put up with the situation.

He had convinced his friend Kirk to help him examine the sensor logs, hoping they would tell them what they wanted to know. But the logs had been erased—an extreme security measure indeed—and the cadets were caught red-handed by Bannock's officers.

Mitchell feared he had thrown their careers into jeopardy, but all they received from Captain Bannock was a reprimand. The worst part of the incident, as it turned out, was that they might never know what had happened to the *Republic* that night.

Now, thought the navigator, that could all change. They could become privy to the mystery. Once again, he felt the old curiosity awakening in him, gnawing at him. . . .

"I'll take this one in the briefing room, too," Augenthaler told Borrik. He turned to the first officer, who was already standing beside him. "Once again, Mr. Hirota, you've got the conn."

"Aye, sir," said Hirota.

Then the captain got up again and entered the turbolift. As the doors closed behind the man, Mitchell cast another look at his friend. Kirk's eyes were burning with a vigor the navigator hadn't seen since the second officer set foot on the *Constitution*.

Mitchell smiled approvingly at the change. Maybe it would soon be like old times after all, he thought. Maybe, despite everything, it would be the way he had imagined it would be.

"Now what?" Lynch wondered out loud.

"Now we learn a little more," Jankowski said hopefully.

Hirota smiled. "Don't bet on it."

The science officer looked at him. "You don't think they're telling the captain more than he knew before?"

"The captain, yes," said the exec. "Us . . . maybe not."

"What makes you say that?" asked Jankowski.

Hirota shrugged. "Experience."

That was when Augenthaler came out of the lift again, just a few short minutes after he had left. The man had an uncharacteristically serious look on his face. Everyone glanced at him, the navigator included, hoping to see how the plot might have thickened.

The captain plunked himself down in his seat and gave Kirk a set of coordinates. To Mitchell's delight, they fell into the part of space he had identified as the *Republic*'s old stomping grounds. The second officer saw it, too; the navigator could tell by the excitement in his friend's expression as he punched in the appropriate data.

"But I have to warn you—we can't do any more speculating about our destination," Augenthaler informed his bridge officers. "This mission is now officially classified."

Lynch and Jankowski didn't seem to like it, but Mitchell wasn't nearly so displeased. To his mind, the "classified" label only underlined the probability that they were going where he thought they were going.

And that, he thought, was a positive development indeed.

As Kirk's shift ended and he saw his replacement approach the helm-navigation console, his mind was still buzzing furiously.

A classified mission, he thought. And it had been assigned to them by Admiral Mangione, of all people.

Admiral Ellen Mangione—it had to be, he mused. The first officer of the *Republic* had surfaced again in his life, still elbow deep in the mystery that had surrounded Kirk's voyage as a second-year cadet. Or so it appeared to the second officer.

One thing was certain—his friend Gary could barely contain himself. As soon as his replacement arrived at the console, the navigator stood up with only minimally disguised eagerness and headed for the turbolift, breezing past the captain's chair.

Kirk was just a step behind him. The lift doors opened and admitted them both with agonizing slowness, then closed again and finally gave them the privacy they had been waiting for.

"Dammit, Jim," said Gary, his voice echoing fiercely in the confines of the lift compartment, "did you hear who that was? Did you hear the captain say her name?"

The second officer nodded. "Mangione," he replied. "Except it seems she's an admiral now."

"Something's happening," his friend commented, punching a destination into the bulkhead unit beside him with more vigor than was absolutely necessary.

"And I'll bet it has to do with that night we spent on the *Republic.*"

Kirk nodded. "It certainly looks that way. I mean, it would be too much of a coincidence otherwise. The question is . . . are we going to find out any more about it than we did before? It looks like they're playing their hand pretty close to the vest."

"Just like before," said Gary over the whirr of the lift motors. "Exactly like before. But we're not cadets anymore, Jim. We're officers now, for petesakes."

The helmsman shook his head. "That's no guarantee. Especially if we happen not to be on the bridge when we reach those coordinates."

His friend looked at him, horrified. "Are you kidding? We've got to be on the bridge. After all these years, I couldn't stand it if we didn't at least get a glimpse of what was going on."

Kirk took a breath, let it out. "Same here," he said. "Now, let's see. If we're traveling at warp six and we've got ten point two light-years between us and those coordinates—"

"That's just under ten days' travel," Gary computed. "So, unless they change the duty schedules on us—"

"We should be right where we want to be—"

"Right when we want to be there," the navigator concluded, completing his friend's thought.

"You know," said Kirk, "we've done our duty. We've kept quiet about what happened on the *Republic* for a long time."

"A long time," Gary agreed.

"We deserve to find out what's going on," the second officer decided.

"And if there's any justice in the world," the navigator added hopefully, "we will."

Kirk nodded. He could hardly wait.

Chapter Eight

NINE DAYS, twenty hours, and forty-one minutes after Captain Augenthaler had recieved his orders from Admiral Mangione, the *Constitution* was slowing to impulse speed and approaching its destination—the outermost planet in a three-planet system.

As Kirk had predicted, he and Gary were on the bridge, tending to their helm and navigation controls respectively. The second officer's pulse raced as he wondered what they would find in the next few moments.

"She's class-M," Lieutenant Lynch said of the red-orange world depicted on their main viewscreen. "But only barely. I wouldn't want to have to eke out an existence on the amount of vegetation that grows there."

"Don't worry," said Augenthaler, "you won't have

124

to." But, bound by his orders, he didn't say anything more.

Kirk wondered if the captain would be sending a team to the planet's surface. It seemed probable that he would. Otherwise, the helmsman thought, why come out all this way?

And if there *was* a landing party, he wanted to be in it. He wanted to see with his own eyes what Bannock and his senior officers had seen that long-ago night on the *Republic*.

"Captain," said Gary.

Kirk glanced at his friend and saw the man's eyes narrowing as he considered the flash of graphics on his monitors. Apparently, something was up.

"What is it, Mr. Mitchell?" asked Augenthaler.

The muscles worked in Gary's jaw. "Sensors show an ion trail, sir. But I can't tell if it's leading toward the planet or away from it."

The second officer peered at the forward viewscreen, but all he saw was the world ahead of them. If the ship that had made the trail was still around, he couldn't find it.

"Mr. Kirk," said Augenthaler, "bring us around the planet. Let's see if that ship is still here."

Barely taking his eyes off the viewscreen, the helmsman did as he was told. His console beeped and the *Constitution* swung around gracefully to starboard, revealing more and more of the planet's hidden side with each passing second.

Finally, Kirk saw something. "There's a ship there, all right." He glanced over his shoulder at the captain.

"Right on the horizon, just a few degrees north of the planet's equator."

As Augenthaler leaned forward in his chair, he squinted his small, blue eyes. "Maximum magnification, Mr. Mitchell."

Gary gave the captain what he asked for. The image on the viewscreen jumped tenfold in size, granting everyone on the bridge a more accurate picture of what they were up against.

The vessel was a lusterless blue in color, angular yet austere-looking, its very posture a statement of belligerence. Its saucer-shaped bridge was mounted on a round nodule, which projected proudly from the ship's main hull on a long, almost fragile-looking neck. Broad, flat wings flared out from the ship's flanks, then tucked down and under to form small but efficient warp plasma nacelles.

The second officer had seen its like before, if only in Academy training exercises. In fact, he imagined, everyone present on the *Constitution*'s bridge had been exposed to it in some form or fashion—and if they hadn't, they certainly should have been.

The ship was, unmistakably and undeniably, a Klingon battle cruiser, D-7 class. And, unlikely as it may have seemed, it was orbiting a planet deep in Federation space.

What was it doing there? Kirk wondered. Promoting another bloody conflict between the Klingons and the Federation like those that had marked their history for the last forty years? Trying to bring the two galactic powers to the brink of war?

Augenthaler swore beneath his breath, his thoughts

probably a lot like his second officer's. "Go to red alert, Mr. Borrik. Mr. Kirk, Mr. Mitchell . . . raise shields and power up the weapons array."

Kirk and Gary moved to comply with the captain's orders, their fingers crawling over their controls like exotic insects as the bridge illumination switched to a lurid crimson. In a matter of moments, the *Constitution* was primed and ready for battle.

Meanwhile, the Klingon vessel had begun wheeling about to face them. But it was doing so slowly, almost elegantly, without any apparent sense of urgency or animosity.

The second officer didn't get it. The battle cruiser was operating at full power, if the *Constitution*'s sensor readouts could be believed. And yet, the enemy wasn't activating its weapons banks or diverting any extra power to its deflector shields.

As far as Kirk could tell, the commander of the Klingon ship had no intention of fighting at all. In fact, he acted as if he had as much right to be there as the starship did. Stranger and stranger, Kirk thought—and the expressions on the faces of his fellow officers told him he wasn't the only one who thought so.

Suddenly, the image of the alien vessel was replaced by another—the face of Admiral Mangione. Kirk recognized her immediately. The woman's hair was grayer than when the second officer had seen it last, but otherwise she hadn't changed a great deal.

Augenthaler got up from his chair and took a step toward the viewscreen. "We're about to close with a

Klingon battle cruiser," he boomed. "I need this screen clear."

"That's exactly what I've contacted you about," Mangione told the captain, her demeanor calm and unhurried. "There will be no confrontation between you and the Klingon."

Augenthaler looked shocked. "What?" he exclaimed.

"You heard me," the admiral said. "Power down your weapons and withdraw from your present coordinates."

Augenthaler shook his head. "Do you know what you're saying? That ship is full of Klingons, for godsakes."

"I know exactly what I'm saying," Mangione insisted, her tone becoming a little steelier. "Now do as I tell you. Power down and get your ship the hell out of there."

If the captain was confused, Kirk was even more so. The Klingons were unprincipled, barbaric, hostile . . . not at all the kind of people you wanted to give free rein on your home turf. Yet one of Starfleet's highest-ranking officers had ordered them to do just that.

The captain frowned deeply. "As you wish," he told the admiral. Turning to Gary with obvious reluctance, he said, "Power down weapons, Mr. Mitchell." Then he addressed Kirk. "Bring us about, Lieutenant."

"Aye, sir," said the helmsman. Working at his controls, he swung the *Constitution* around 180 degrees.

But there was no starfield streaming by on the

forward viewscreen to corroborate Kirk's sensor readings. The screen still displayed Mangione's stern, gray-haired visage.

Augenthaler regarded her. "I don't suppose you care to tender an explanation," he ventured.

"I do not," said the admiral.

"Figures," Gary muttered, speaking loudly enough for Kirk to hear him but no one else.

"As I mentioned earlier, Captain," Mangione continued, "this matter has been classified top priority by Starfleet Command under General Order Nine. In accordance with that designation, I'm imposing a permanent order of silence—not only on you, but also on your bridge officers and anyone else who had knowledge of the Klingons' presence here."

Out of the corner of his eye, the second officer saw his friend glance at him pointedly. He didn't return the gesture.

"No one is to speak of this or refer to it in any way," Mangione elaborated, "either in public or in private, unless and until you're advised otherwise by a member of the executive council. As far as you're concerned, the incident never took place. Is this clear?"

Augenthaler and his bridge officers hesitated for a moment. Then there was a chorus of reluctant affirmatives.

"Good," said the admiral. "Mangione out."

Finally, her image vanished from the screen. Kirk and the others looked to the captain, who had turned an angry shade of red.

"You heard the lady," Augenthaler told them dutifully, though he clearly didn't like having to say it. "As far as you're concerned, none of this ever happened."

The second officer turned back to his control panel and sighed. After all, he had heard those orders before.

Mitchell scanned the rec lounge to make sure no one was listening in on his conversation. Then he leaned across the table and waited until his friend looked up from his meal.

"So," he asked softly, too low for anyone to eavesdrop, "what do you think happened out there?"

Kirk frowned, making no effort to hide his disappointment. "We're not supposed to talk about this," he replied. "I'd say Admiral Mangione made that pretty clear."

"Give me a break," the navigator told him, his voice becoming a shade harsher as he pled his case. "We're human beings, aren't we? Even if we can't let anyone else in on what happened, we can talk about it among ourselves. Hell, we have to. Otherwise, we'll go nuts."

The second officer frowned. "We're Starfleet officers. We're supposed to follow orders."

"And we do," Mitchell argued, "when they're even remotely reasonable, which this one isn't."

Kirk appeared to weigh his friend's position. Finally, he spoke up again. "I suppose there isn't any harm in it," he concluded, "as long as it's just you and me."

The navigator made a fist and bounced it lightly off

the table for emphasis. "Damned right there isn't any harm in it."

"Still," said the second officer, "what's there to say? We saw a Klingon ship in Federation space. It's a—"

Abruptly, Kirk stopped himself. There was a crewman walking in their direction.

Only when the man was well past them did Kirk start up again. "It's a mystery," he allowed. "No question about it. But we'll probably never come close to solving it."

"Not true," said Mitchell yielding to an antic impulse. "We could always wait until the captain's asleep and access the ship's sensor logs."

Kirk looked at him, his features pinched in a mixture of trepidation and disbelief. It was only after he came to the realization that his friend was joking that he began to relax again.

Mitchell smiled a sly smile. "Admit it. I had you going for a second there," he noted.

"For a second," the second officer conceded, closing his eyes and massaging his temples with his fingers.

"Actually," said the junior officer, "I wish it were as easy as accessing some logs. In this case, we'd probably have to break into Starfleet Headquarters to find out what's going on."

Kirk regarded him more closely. "You still think this has something to do with what happened that night on the *Republic?*"

"Don't you?" Mitchell asked in return.

"More than ever," the other man replied.

Going over the possibilities, the navigator frowned.

"So what do you think it is?" he wondered. "An exchange of hostages? A battle cruiser full of double agents?" He leaned in more closely. "Or maybe a secret alliance with the Klingons, stretching back who knows how many years?"

Kirk shook his head emphatically. "None of the above—especially the last one. The Klingons are too vicious, too hungry for power. The Federation would never align itself with an entity it couldn't trust."

Mitchell snorted. "Really? It looked to me like Mangione was willing enough to trust them."

"An isolated incident," Kirk argued.

"Or two," his friend reminded him. "Or maybe more than two. Maybe more than a hundred. I mean . . . who knows how many times this kind of thing has happened before and been hushed over?"

"Not us," Kirk conceded.

The remark took the wind out of Mitchell's sails. "Not us," he was forced to agree.

Ultimately, he supposed, they might never learn the truth of the matter. They might never find out what a Klingon battle cruiser was doing in Federation space, or why a Starfleet admiral had commanded the *Constitution* to back off from it—much less why they had been ordered to go there in the first place.

It killed the navigator to think that way, but he had to face facts. Whatever had been going on in the vicinity of that red-orange world would probably continue to go on forever, and Admiral Mangione's secret would remain just that . . . a secret.

In fact, only one good thing had come out of the incident—Mitchell's friend had begun to emerge from his shell. He had begun to act a little like the Kirk the navigator knew at the Academy.

And hell, he thought, wasn't that more important than whether or not they uncovered some stodgy old Starfleet mystery?

Kang, son of K'naiah, strode the broad central corridor of the Klingon vessel *Stormwind,* acutely aware of the warriors he passed going in the opposite direction—and in particular, the expressions on their faces.

After all, one or more of those warriors might have been coming from the captain's quarters, and that was where Kang was headed at the moment. It was always good to get some inkling of the captain's mood before one imposed oneself upon his presence.

Unfortunately, no one whose face he searched seemed particularly distracted. No one looked as if he or she had been congratulated or rebuked or threatened or encouraged. They simply had the look of Klingons going about their daily business.

Not helpful, thought Kang. Not helpful at all.

He wished dearly to know why the captain had summoned him. Certainly, he had earned himself something of a reputation for arrogance, but that was hardly an offense among his people. In fact, some would say it was a quality well worth cultivating.

A moment later, Kang came in sight of Captain Ibrach's quarters. There was a single guard posted outside—a very large, very powerful warrior named Anyoqq, who eyed Kang as he approached.

It wasn't just Anyoqq's size that made him so

fearsome-looking. It was also the oversized disruptor pistol tucked into his belt and the long, deadly dagger whose hilt protruded from his boot top.

But Kang didn't allow himself to be intimidated. Instead, he stopped in front of the giant, looked up confidently into his broad, bony face and said, "The captain has summoned me."

Anyoqq regarded him with his tiny black eyes as if he were thinking about pulling Kang's arms and legs off one by one. Then he gave a hard rap with his mighty knuckles on Captain Ibrach's door.

The captain's reponse came through an intercom grid built into the bulkhead beside his door. "What is it?" he rasped.

The giant pointed to Kang. "Your name," he demanded.

"Kang, son of K'naiah," said the youth.

Anyoqq glanced at the intercom grid for a second. Finally, Ibrach replied. "Send him in," he said.

The giant stepped aside and jerked his big, scarred thumb in the direction of the door. "Go," he rumbled.

Kang didn't wait to be told twice. As the door slid aside for him, he entered the captain's anteroom.

Ibrach was seated on a heavy metal chair with furs strewn across it. A disruptor pistol lay on one of its armrests, mere inches from the captain's hand. After all, the life expectancy of a Klingon commander was directly proportional to the ambition of his officers, and the *Stormwind* was known to have some ambitious officers indeed.

"Kang," said Ibrach, a broad-shouldered man with

long, gray hair that fell around his shoulders and a thick, drooping mustache.

The younger warrior slammed his fist against the left side of his chest, just above his hearts. "My captain."

Ibrach eyed him from beneath his prominent brow ridge. "I understand you have been demanding things from your superiors," he said.

Kang straightened. "I have."

The commander's lip curled beneath his mustache. "You have made it known you do not like traveling through Federation territory on a mission you know nothing about."

"That is true," Kang told him.

"You wish to be let in on the mystery."

"True again," Kang conceded.

Ibrach leaned forward in his seat, his lips pulling back to expose his teeth. "And who are you to make demands?" he roared, his voice echoing savagely from bulkhead to bulkhead. "Who gave you the authority?"

The younger Klingon stood his ground. "I am Kang," he answered evenly, "son of K'naiah, and I ask permission of no one when my rights as a warrior have been trampled on."

"Rights?" the captain spat, his voice dripping with disdain. "Of what rights do you speak?"

Kang didn't back down. "A warrior must hold his honor higher than anything," he insisted, "even higher than the predator who wheels in the heavens. But how can he know whether he follows the path of honor if his destination is shrouded in secrecy?"

Ibrach lifted his chin. "In other words, you distrust my motives? You think I'm conspiring with the Federation?"

"I distrust nothing," said Kang, "and everything, until the facts are set before me."

"You," the commander sneered, "who are little more than a mewling child?" He pounded his scarred, thick-knuckled fist on his armrest, coming within a half-inch of his weapon. "You wish to be privy to that which is spoken of in a captain's councils?"

The younger warrior felt a flash of righteous anger. "I am no child," he growled menacingly. "I am a warrior, my lord. If you have the slightest doubt about that—"

Ibrach held up his hand for silence. He glared at Kang for a moment. Then he did something that caught the younger Klingon completely off guard. He threw back his gray-haired head and laughed.

It was a loud laugh, a deep laugh. It resounded from one wall to the next, filling the room with its savage mirth. Kang hesitated, not knowing what to make of it.

"You mock me?" he asked.

"Far from it," said his superior. "I applaud you, son of K'naiah. My officers told me about a whelp who yielded to no one, but I had to see him with my own eyes." He pointed to the younger man with a gnarled finger. "I had to witness his bravado for myself."

Kang regarded him. "Then you will tell me of our mission?" he wondered, daring to hope it was true.

Ibrach grunted. "I will. After all, it is the sort of mission that must be carried out time and again, and you are a warrior who will have a command of his own one day."

The younger Klingon shook his head from side to side. "I do not understand," he was forced to admit.

"Not yet, you don't," his commander replied, his eyes narrowing with the promise of intrigue. "But you will, Kang. You will. . . ."

Chapter Nine

VODIS VODANIS stood at the rail of his office's wide, curved balcony and looked out over the capital city of his planet. It was an exhilarating experience, to say the least.

Elegant new buildings were rising everywhere, pristine pink and white towers and pale blue domes taking the place of the older, darker edifices that had been ravaged in the bad times five years earlier. Vodanis raised his face to the sun and smiled, basking in the knowledge that such a tragedy would never befall his people again.

Now their plentiful mineral resources would go toward the funding of more housing, more cultural programs, and more assistance for the needy. Their planet's wealth wouldn't be leached from it by pirates and plunderers, bringing misery and destruction to their civilization in the process.

And why would they be spared further hardships? Because he and his counselors had seen the wisdom of joining the United Federation of Planets, a union of many different species with a single worthwhile goal—the advancement of science, trade, and culture.

Some among his people had warned Vodanis not to place his trust in the aliens, no matter how benign they might seem. After all, no Sordinian had ever benefited from contact with offworlders.

But Vodanis, who had been elected his people's Prime mere months before the Federation's first overture, followed his instincts above all. He welcomed the organization's diplomatic envoys with open arms. He came to understand them and helped them to understand the Sordinians. And in the end, he saw to it that his world became an equal partner in the alliance.

These days, no one challenged the wisdom of the Prime's decision any longer. After all, the Federation had done everything it said it would do for Sordinia IV. Except for one thing, of course—it never sent combat vessels to rescue the planet from pirates.

But then, it had never needed to. Since Vodanis's world was accepted into the Federation, it hadn't received a single visit from an alien force bent on plundering. Clearly, such visitors had been daunted by the reputation of the Sordinians' new friends.

The Prime smiled. His people's situation had not been so stable, so promising, in a hundred years, and he had had a hand in making it that way. It was a gratifying thought, to say the least.

A hawk began circling one of the newest towers, as if looking for prey. Vodanis was studying it when he heard a short, shrill sound that originated inside his office. It was the sound of his communications device, alerting him to a caller.

Vodanis felt his pulse speed up as he went inside to respond. It had to be his daughter on the line, he told himself. She had reached the final stage of the capital's annual visual-arts competition, and the winner was to be announced that morning.

The Prime hoped that his child had attained the top prize. She had worked so hard on her project, sometimes waking up in the middle of the night to make some small change or addition to it. It would be a great injustice, he reflected, if she were to fall short of her goal.

But then, Vodanis reminded himself, it would have been an even greater injustice if his daughter had never had the chance to pursue her calling—like so many young artists who had grown up during one alien invasion or another. If nothing else, he mused, at least his child had been raised in an era of peace and plenty.

If she won, he would be happy for her. But if she lost, it would not be the end of the world. He would remind her that there would be another competition the following year.

Sitting at his desk and pressing a stud on his communications device, the Prime said, "This is Vodanis."

But it wasn't his daughter's image that greeted him on his desk monitor. It was the image of his security minister, a heavyset individual with a long, proud braid. And unless the Prime was sorely mistaken, the man seemed frantic about something.

"Prime Vodanis," Reggis heaved, barely able to catch his breath, "they are back! For the love of serenity . . ." He pulled out a cloth and dabbed at the perspiration on his forehead.

Vodanis felt an all-too-familiar weight on the back of his neck. No, he thought, experiencing a bit of panic. Reggis can't mean that. He must be speaking of something else.

"Who is back?" he forced himself to say.

The security minister swallowed. "The aliens, Prime—they have returned! You must alert our friends in the Federation!"

Feeling the weight on his neck getting heavier, Vodanis leaned closer to the monitor. "The aliens . . . ? But surely, they know we are no longer alone . . . no longer defenseless . . ."

"If they know," said Reggis, "they do not seem to care. You must contact the Federation, Prime, before it is too late!"

Vodanis was hardly any less agitated than his security minister. However, he had to have more information before he could consider sending a message to their allies. He had to understand the nature of the threat.

"How many ships?" he asked Reggis. "How close?"

The security minister shook his head. "You misapprehend me, Prime. They are not ships."

141

Vodanis straightened. "Not ships...? But then—"

Reggis held his hand up, cloth and all, and did his best to keep his explanation brief. When he was done, the Prime realized that his minister was right to be so frantic. The threat he described might have been the most dangerous the Sordinians had ever faced.

And as he had indicated, there were no ships.

"I will contact Starbase Twenty-three," Vodanis said reassuringly. "They will dispatch someone to help us, Reggis."

His minister sighed. "I am sure they will, Prime. I just hope that help arrives in time."

Inwardly, Vodanis couldn't help echoing the sentiment.

Kirk had barely begun his shift at the *Constitution*'s helm when he heard Lieutenant Borrik address the captain. As Augenthaler turned around in response, so did the second officer and his friend Gary.

"I have a communication for you from Starbase Twenty-three," said the Dedderac. "Apparently, sir, we have new orders."

Since Admiral Mangione sent them packing a day earlier, the *Constitution* had embarked on a long-overdue security sweep of her sector. Of course, Kirk had known that new orders would come down eventually, but he hadn't expected it to happen so soon.

Apparently, neither had Augenthaler. He scowled at Borrik. "Don't tell me, Lieutenant. Eyes only, right?"

The Dedderac showed his teeth, which was as close

as he would ever come to a smile. "Actually, sir, it's an unrestricted communication. I can put it on the viewscreen, if you like."

The captain grunted, a little surprised. "By all means. It'll be refreshing to speak to someone from the comfort of my bridge again."

A moment later, the image of a Starfleet admiral appeared on the screen. But it wasn't Ellen Mangione. It was a bald, gray-bearded man whom Kirk had never seen before.

"Admiral Blosser," said Augenthaler. "To what do we owe the pleasure of this communication?"

The admiral smiled a wan smile. "It's not a pleasure at all, I'm afraid. Are you familiar with Sordinia Four, Captain?"

"Of course," Augenthaler responded. "It's a Federation member-planet just a few light-years from here. What's the matter?"

Blosser sighed. "A handful of satellites have suddenly shown up in orbit around the planet. The origin of the satellites is unknown, but the Sordinians believe they're a prelude to invasion—particularly because their world is so rich in hard-to-find mineral resources."

"And what does Starfleet think?" the captain inquired.

Kirk was wondering the same thing.

"We don't know," said the admiral. "That's why we're dispatching the *Constitution*. If you find that these satellites are threats to the security of Sordinia Four, you're authorized to do whatever you deem necessary to get rid of them."

"And if we find they're benign?" asked Augenthaler.

"Then you'll have to find a way to convince the Sordinians of it. You see, they tend to be a little . . . nervous, given their experiences before joining the Federation. If I had a credit for every time they've been plundered in the last fifty years, I'd have a fortune."

The captain nodded. "I understand."

"I'm glad," said the admiral. "Keep me posted on the situation, will you? Blosser out."

As the older man's image vanished from the viewscreen, Augenthaler turned to Gary. "Chart a course to Sordinia Four, Mr. Mitchell."

"Aye, sir," said the navigator as he got to work.

The captain glanced at Kirk. "Warp six, Lieutenant."

"Warp six, sir," the helmsman acknowledged.

They had a mission, he noted inwardly. True, it wasn't the mission that would have told them what happened that night on the *Republic,* when he and his fellow cadets were confined to their quarters.

But at least it was something to keep his ghosts at bay.

As Mitchell looked up from his navigational controls to scan the bridge's forward viewscreen, he stole another glance at his friend.

Fortunately, Kirk seemed to have rejoined the ranks of the living. There was a glint in his eye and a lift to his chin that the navigator hadn't seen since the second officer beamed aboard the *Constitution*, and they were welcome sights indeed.

Of course, Mitchell would have felt even better if Kirk had opened up and told him what was on his mind. But Rome wasn't built in a day, or so he'd heard. Having seen some improvement in his friend's demeanor, he could find it in himself to be patient and let events unfold at their own pace.

Just as the junior officer came to that conclusion, he saw a crimson blip on one of his monitors. Swiveling in his chair to face Captain Augenthaler, he said, "Sir? I have Sordinia Four on short-range sensors."

The captain nodded. "Let's see 'er, Mr. Mitchell."

The navigator did as his commanding officer asked. A moment later, the blue-green disk of Sordinia IV appeared on the viewscreen, backlit by the yellow blaze of its sun.

Out of the corner of his eye, Mitchell saw his friend Jim studying the planet with undisguised curiosity, the glare of the viewscreen reflected in his eyes. It was another welcome sign that the old Jim Kirk was beginning to emerge again.

Augenthaler leaned forward in his center seat. "Can you show me where those satellites are, Mr. Mitchell?"

The navigator punched a command into his black control panel, asking the sensors to pinpoint the locations of the items in question. He was barely finished before three yellow computer blips appeared on the viewscreen against the backdrop of Sordinia IV.

"There they are," said Mitchell.

"So it would seem," the captain replied. He leaned forward and squinted at the screen. "From here, they appear to be spaced at regular intervals. Can you confirm that for me, Mr. Lynch?"

"Yes, sir, I can," said the science officer, having already collected that information from his monitors. He looked up from his console. "And if that's the case, sir, there are very likely additional satellites orbiting on the far side of the planet."

"The Sordinians mentioned six in all," Augenthaler recalled. "Magnify one of them, Mr. Mitchell."

"Aye, sir," said the navigator. His console chirped as he worked.

The yellow computer blips vanished. Then the blue-green disk appeared to jump closer to them, revealing what seemed like a tiny object floating in space above it. The thing was black and more or less hourglass-shaped, with a collection of unidentified devices protruding from its top, its bottom, and its narrow waist.

"Is it manned, Mr. Lynch?" the captain asked.

"Hard to tell," the science officer answered. "There's a forcefield around it that's playing havoc with our sensors, sir. The only good reading we can get is a visual one."

"Hail it, Mr. Borrik," said Augenthaler.

Mitchell turned to watch the communications officer comply with the order. "No answer," Borrik responded after a moment or two.

The captain turned to Lynch. "Care to speculate as to what these things might be, Lieutenant?"

The science officer frowned in the red glow of his monitors. "They could be almost anything, sir."

"I don't see any weapons batteries," Kirk chipped in.

"No obvious ones," said Augenthaler, his brow furrowing. "But that doesn't mean the things aren't armed. They could have weapons concealed inside them, ready to roll out at the first sign of trouble."

"Or they could be completely innocuous," Lynch suggested. "Maybe a prelude to first contact."

"You mean someone's examining the Sordinians before they initiate relations?" the captain asked.

"That's what I'm thinking," said the science officer.

Mitchell saw Augenthaler scowl and turn in his chair. "It's certainly a possibility. Mr. Borrik, hail Prime Vodanis. Let's see if he can shed any more light on the situation for us."

"Aye, sir," said the Dedderac. He carried out the order, then looked up. "I have Prime Vodanis, Captain."

Augenthaler faced forward again and got up from his chair. "On screen."

A moment later, the Sordinian's image appeared on the viewscreen. Vodanis was a tall and bony individual with eyes the color of silver, skin as glossy and dark as an eggplant's, and a long mane of fine, white hair gathered into an elaborate braid.

He was also the highest elected leader of the Sordinian worldwide government, which represented the planet's eleven billion inhabitants. Mitchell had read about the Prime between shifts, in the privacy of his quarters. The Starfleet file had described Vodanis's courage and perseverance in the face of considerable adversity.

Unfortunately, the fellow didn't look very courageous on the viewscreen. In fact, he looked pretty shaken up.

And Vodanis was the leader of his civilization, Mitchell mused. If he was reacting to the satellites in a bad way, the other Sordinians must have been quaking in their boots.

"I am pleased to see you, Captain," the Prime told Augenthaler, his voice trembling ever so slightly. He swallowed visibly. "Believe me, you don't know how happy."

"Has something happened?" asked the captain. "Have the satellites made any threatening moves?"

"None," the Prime replied. "At least, not yet. However, my people are certain we will soon be attacked by them, and that feeling has unleashed a worldwide panic. I have seen madness and terrible violence, and it only promises to get worse."

Vodanis planted three-fingered hands on the surface in front of him and leaned closer to the viewscreen. There was a decidedly desperate look in his large, silver eyes.

"Captain Augenthaler," he said, "we have never devoted our planet's resources to the making of weapons. We are unprepared to deal with these satellites. But you—"

"We have weapons," Augenthaler responded, following the obvious logic of the Sordinian's remarks.

Vodanis nodded. "Yes, my friend. You have weapons. And you must use them to end the danger to us."

If there is a danger, Mitchell thought. To that point, no one had established anything one way or the other.

The captain took a breath, let it out. "We'll do whatever we can, Prime Vodanis. Augenthaler out."

A moment later the Sordinian's image vanished from the screen, to be replaced by the same blue-green sweep of his world that the second officer had seen before. The satellite loomed a little larger, however, one sleek surface glinting in the sunlight.

Studying the thing for a while, Augenthaler sat down again in his chair and tapped his fingers on his armrest. Finally, he spoke up. "Hail it again, Mr. Borrik," he told his Dedderac communications officer.

Borrik hailed it. As before, there was no answer.

The captain grunted. "Either the damned thing is automated or whoever's inside it just doesn't want to talk."

Hirota came over to stand by Augenthaler's center seat. "We've got to do something," he told the captain.

Augenthaler nodded. "You can say that again, Commander. Unfortunately, we can't just blast these satellites out of the sky. What if it turns out they're occupied after all?"

"A good question," the first officer conceded. "On the other hand, we can't allow matters on Sordinia Four to spiral out of control. The Sordinians' panic could do more damage to them than any enemy."

The captain looked at him. "What do you suggest?"

Mitchell wanted to know as well.

Hirota shrugged. "Maybe the two of us should go

down there and hold Vodanis's hand for a while—show the Sordinians that we're not going to let anything bad happen to them."

"You could do that from the ship, sir," Lynch reminded Augenthaler.

His eyes still locked on the viewscreen, the captain shook his head. "No, Lieutenant, I think Commander Hirota had it right. We need to do this in person. Show the Sordinians that we're not afraid to be down there with them."

He looked around the bridge at his officers, Mitchell included. "Besides, all we can do for now is continue studying the satellites—and this staff is perfectly capable of doing that without a captain and a first officer. In fact, we'd probably only get in the way."

Hirota smiled. "Not probably, sir."

Augenthaler seemed to consider it a moment longer. Then he got up from his center seat again and regarded his second officer. "Mr. Kirk," he announced, "you've got the conn."

Kirk swiveled in his seat. "Aye, sir."

The captain pulled down on the front of his uniform shirt. "Commander Hirota and I will be beaming down to Prime Vodanis's office. If you run into any trouble, contact us there."

Kirk nodded. "Acknowledged, sir."

Augenthaler led the way to the turbolift with Hirota on his heels. The doors opened with a soft whoosh and engulfed them, then closed again.

Mitchell glanced at his friend. Kirk seemed to notice, because he glanced back at him.

"Your orders, sir?" the navigator inquired in the most respectful voice he could manage.

The second officer frowned disapprovingly. "Let's get someone up here to man the helm," he said.

"Right away, sir," Mitchell assured him.

This was going to be a good thing, he told himself, as he called for a backup helmsman via the ship's intercom system. The more responsibility his friend had, the less he would think about whatever was bothering him.

Yes, the junior officer thought, stealing another glance at Kirk. It would be a very good thing.

Kirk waited until he saw Medina, his backup, come through the turbolift doors. Then he stood up, relinquished his post to the new helmsman, and turned to the empty seat just behind him.

It was a short-backed, metallic, blockish-looking affair with broad, sturdy armrests and a dark sheen to it, resting on a platform just a bit higher than the rest of the command center. And at one time, it had been the symbol of everything to which he aspired in life.

Back at the Academy, Kirk had played commanding officer in plenty of computer-generated simulations—too many to count, in fact—and in each of those simulations, he had given his virtual crew their orders from a captain's chair. But all the while, he had yearned to sit in a real captain's chair on the bridge of a real starship.

Of course, being a junior officer, he had never been placed in charge of a real ship. It wasn't until the *Farragut* was plunged into nightmare that Kirk found himself the ranking officer on a Starfleet vessel—and at the time, he was too busy at the helm to even think of sitting in the chair that had been Captain Garrovick's.

Now things were different. It wasn't circumstances that had given him the center seat. It was Augenthaler—and he had done it of his own free will. Finally, the second officer's wish had been granted.

But how much did it mean to him now? As much as it might have meant a year or two earlier? Or had his experience on the *Farragut* forever stolen his yearning to command?

Kirk wasn't sure. But he knew this—he had been ordered to look after the *Constitution* while his captain was away. His feelings about the situation were secondary; he would see his duty done.

Stepping up to the captain's chair, he turned around and deposited himself in it. As it turned out, the thing wasn't any more comfortable than it looked. A saying occurred to him: Heavy lies the head that wears the crown.

Kirk wasn't a king any more than the *Constitution* was a kingdom, but the analogy seemed apt nonetheless. One wasn't supposed to get comfortable in the center seat. One was supposed to tolerate it, even learn to adapt to it—but never really relax in it.

Not when so much depended on one's alertness. Not when the safety of ship and crew hung in the balance of every decision.

For a moment, the second officer saw the bridge of the *Farragut* superimposed over the *Constitution*'s.

He saw the bodies of the command staff lying where they had fallen, their faces deathly pale and cold to the touch. He wanted to look away, but the corpses were everywhere, draped over chairs and slumped at the bases of consoles. . . .

He closed his eyes tight. When he opened them, the corpses were gone. There was no one there but his bridge officers.

Kirk looked around to see if anyone had noticed his discomfort. As far as he could tell, no one had—not even Gary. Everyone was simply going about his or her business.

As the second officer sat back in his chair, shaken but relieved, he heard the turbolift doors whisper open behind him. Out of curiosity, he glanced at the lift—and saw that it was Lieutenant Gaynor.

What's more, Gaynor glanced back at him—then stopped dead in his tracks. He stared at Kirk for a second or two, his expression a mixture of resentment and disbelief. *You,* he seemed to say, *in that chair?* Then, with what seemed like an effort, he tore his eyes off the second officer and proceeded to the empty security console along the port bulkhead.

"I have the transporter room," Borrik announced.

Kirk turned to him. "And?"

"Apparently," said the communications officer, "the captain and Commander Hirota arrived safely in the Sordinian capital."

The second officer nodded. "Good."

He eyed the viewscreen, with its image of one of the alien satellites. The object seemed so peaceful floating there in space, so unassuming. But as Kirk had learned all too well, the most benign-looking things could turn out to be the deadliest.

The second officer had barely completed his thought when he saw a beam of blue-white fire leap from the satellite to the planet's surface. It happened so quickly, so unexpectedly, he thought for a moment that it might have been his imagination.

"What was that?" he asked.

Another bolt of blue-white energy left the satellite. And another. His mouth went dry.

Finally, Gary answered him. "The satellite is firing on the capital," he said, unable to mask the surprise in his voice.

Kirk looked at his friend, trying to absorb the information. The alien satellite was just what the Sordinians had feared, it seemed—the tool of an aggressor. But now that the second officer knew that, now that he had seen it with his own eyes . . . what was he going to do about it?

Remembering his orders, he turned to the Dedderac. "Contact the captain," he said as calmly as he could.

"Aye, sir," Borrik responded.

Kirk saw another bolt of blue-white energy descend from the satellite to the planet. *If the captain doesn't respond in another couple of seconds,* he thought, *I'm going to have to—*

"I have Captain Augenthaler," the communications officer announced.

"On screen," said the second officer.

A moment later, Augenthaler's ruddy face filled the

viewscreen. "Dammit," he rasped, "what's going on up there, Lieutenant?"

Kirk got up from his chair. "One of the orbital stations has begun firing at you, sir."

"You didn't do anything to trigger this?" asked the captain.

The second officer shook his head. "No, sir. I—" Abruptly, something occurred to him. "Unless the satellite detected our transporter beam . . . and was programmed to react to it."

Captain Augenthaler frowned. "That's a possibility, I suppose. In any case, we've got a problem on our hands. The Sordinians have energy shields in place to protect the capital, but they won't be able to hold up under this kind of barrage for long."

As if to punctuate his words, there was a flash of white light in the background. With Sordinians running back and forth, their voices strident with urgency, Augenthaler muttered a curse.

"And of course," he went on, "neither Commander Hirota nor I can beam back to the *Constitution* until the Sordinians lower their shields—so it's up to you to disable the satellite, Mr. Kirk."

The second officer nodded. "Acknowledged, sir."

"Step lively, man," said the captain. "Augenthaler out."

Kirk glanced at his bridge officers. "Shields up," he told them. "Battle stations."

Everyone began to move at the same time. Fingers flew over slick, black control panels. Monitors flashed. Consoles conspired to create a symphony of high-pitched sounds.

The second officer turned to Gaynor, who was still standing beside the security station. "Power up our weapons, Lieutenant."

Despite his feelings about the younger man, the security officer did as he was instructed. "Weapons powered up and ready," he announced crisply after a second or two.

Kirk eyed his replacement at the helm. "Move to within five hundred meters of the satellite, Mr. Medina."

"Aye, sir," said Medina.

The *Constitution* edged closer to its target. In a matter of seconds, it had obtained the desired range.

"Target phasers and fire," the second officer commanded.

Twin shafts of seething, orange energy shot out from the starship's forward weapons ports, punching holes in the alien satellite's defenses and ravaging its outer hull. What's more, the beams raking the capital disappeared in an explosion of blue-white energy.

No doubt Gaynor had hit the satellite's weapons center. *Objective accomplished,* Kirk thought.

Then something happened that he hadn't anticipated. There was an impact that made the deck slide and shudder beneath his feet. He looked to Gary at navigation. "Report," he demanded.

"Shields down twenty percent," the navigator said. Then he added, "It's the other satellites on this side of the planet. They started firing on us as soon as we activated our phasers."

The second officer felt the deck jerk again, forcing him to grab the captain's chair or lose his footing. As

Gary announced that their shields were down forty-five percent, Kirk glared at the satellite they'd been firing on and tried to get a handle on the situation.

Obviously, he concluded, the satellites were linked somehow. When one of them was attacked, the others were programmed to defend it. It was a level of coordination neither the second officer nor Captain Augenthaler had been prepared for.

"Try to jam their signals," Kirk told Borrik.

The Dedderac made the attempt. But after a moment or two, his console emitted a high-pitched sound and he shook his long, striped head. "It's not working, sir," he reported. "They're protecting the signal from me somehow."

"Lieutenant," Lynch called out, "three of the other satellites have begun firing on the capital as well."

They were picking up the slack left by the first satellite, Kirk realized. So, really, he hadn't accomplished anything at all with his phaser barrage. In fact, he had unwittingly made matters worse.

"Contact Captain Augenthaler," he told Borrik.

The Dedderac worked for a moment at his console. Finally, he looked up and said, "Sorry, sir."

The second officer turned to him. "Sorry?"

"The energy barrage is interfering with my signal," Borrik explained. "I can't get through to the capitol."

Kirk cursed beneath his breath. Clearly, he was on his own. "Keep trying," he ordered, just in case.

"What do you want the rest of us to do?" asked Gaynor, a touch of mockery in the man's voice.

Good question, the second officer thought. A third

time, he felt the deck lurch beneath him, nearly throwing him to the floor despite his hold on the center seat.

Gary swiveled in his chair to look back at him. "Shields down fifty-five percent, sir."

If he waited any longer, Kirk told himself, some critical system would be disabled and the ship would be rendered helpless. Better to retreat now, while he still had all his options open.

"Get us out of here," he told Medina. "Full impulse."

"Aye, sir," said the helmsman, implementing his orders.

The second officer saw the satellite dwindle in size as the *Constitution* withdrew precipitously from the vicinity. He could sense his bridge officers breathing a collective sigh of relief.

But what about Augenthaler and Hirota, down on the planet's surface? And what about everyone else in the capital? How long could they hold out against three barrages at once?

Kirk looked around at his bridge personnel. At the Academy, he'd had a professor who told him a captain's greatest resource was his command staff. He decided to test that theory.

Tapping a stud on his armrest, he accessed the intercom system. "Lieutenant Jankowski, Dr. Velasquez . . . this is Lieutenant Kirk. I need you up on the bridge on the double."

Less than two minutes later, the doctor and the chief engineer emerged from the turbolift and took their places at the red-orange rail that surrounded the command center. The second officer regarded them along with Lynch, Gaynor, Medina, Borrik, and his friend Gary.

"All right," he told them, his voice cracking like a whip in the close environs of the bridge. "I need options and I need them *now*."

Chapter Ten

"WELL?" Kirk prodded.

Finally, Lynch sighed and took the lead. "Obviously," he observed, "we can't go back in and pick off the satellites one by one. Not when they're programmed to respond in concert."

"Absolutely," Jankowski chimed in. "We need another option."

"There's got to be a way to keep the stations from working together," Gary asserted. He frowned as he weighed the possibilities. "Maybe we can screw up their communications protocols."

"Yes," said Gaynor skeptically, "but how? We've already tried to jam their signals without any success."

No one seemed to have an alternative in mind. Kirk

racked his brain, but he couldn't come up with one either.

"We're operating in the dark," Velasquez pointed out. "We need to know more about the stations and how they work . . . together and separately. That's the only way we're going to make any headway."

Borrik held up a long, striped finger. "If I may point something out . . ." he began.

"Please do," said Kirk.

"According to my sensor data," the Dedderac told them, "the station we assaulted earlier is extremely vulnerable. Its shields are operating at forty-two percent of capacity."

"That low . . . after one strike?" said Lynch.

"That low," Borrik confirmed.

Kirk stroked his chin. "In other words," he concluded, "with a little more effort, those shields could be eliminated altogether."

"Damned right," said Velasquez. "And with the satellite's shields out of order, our computers can download its operations profile."

"Not necessarily," the Dedderac pointed out.

"Why not?" asked Gary.

Borrik gestured toward one of the monitors, where a red and black graphic indicated the opposition's locations. "These satellites have surprised us more than once already. Who knows what will happen when we link our computers to theirs? Maybe it's the *Constitution*'s files that will be downloaded."

Kirk nodded, seeing the sense in the remark. "The lieutenant's right. We can't risk it."

"Of course," said Borrik, "there is another way."

"What are you suggesting?" asked Lynch, eyeing the Dedderac from across the bridge.

"He's talking about a reconnaissance team," Gary interjected. He looked at the communications officer again. "Isn't he?"

"That is correct," said Borrik. "Once the station's shields are down, we must beam a team over and download the data onsite, then transmit it to our computers. That is the surest and safest way to obtain the information we require."

Kirk nodded to show his understanding. "And when we've got the information in hand, we'll know what steps to take next."

Gary leaned back in his chair. "Of course," he noted, "we'll have to get within forty thousand kilometers of the station to effect a transport."

"And we'll have to drop our shields," Jankowski added soberly. "That means leaving ourselves open to the stations' energy weapons."

"It'll only be for a few seconds," the second officer pointed out.

Lynch grunted. "From what we've seen, those stations can do a hell of a lot of damage in a few seconds."

The science officers' words echoing in their ears, the bridge contingent considered the danger. As before, the only sounds were the low throb of the engines and the warbling of the consoles.

Finally, Kirk spoke up. "It sounds like an acceptable risk," he told the others. "Especially when you consider the increasing severity of the situation in the capital."

Jankowski, on the other hand, didn't seem so sure. She looked at Lynch, who looked at Velasquez, who looked at Borrik. Had Captain Augenthaler made the very same decision, they would no doubt have placed their confidence in it. But an untried and untested second officer . . . that was a different story entirely, and Kirk knew it.

He needed a vote of affirmation—and not just from a lieutenant j.g. with even less experience than he had. He needed one of Augenthaler's veterans to step forward and support his plan.

One did.

"The man's right," said Gaynor. "We need to move quickly, and this is as good a strategy as any."

Velasquez frowned. "Jack . . . there's no telling what a landing party will encounter on that station."

"True," the security chief replied forcefully. "But isn't that why we all signed on with Starfleet in the first place?" He jerked a thumb over his shoulder at the viewscreen. "To explore the unknown? To encounter things no one has encountered before?"

Once the problem was placed in that light, it was hard for anyone to argue with Kirk's decision. In fact, Jankowski broke into a grin.

"Count me in," she said.

Lynch nodded. "Me, too."

"What the hell," Velasquez added. "It's unanimous."

"I'll remind you that this is not a democracy," said Kirk. "Nonetheless, I appreciate your support."

He glanced at Gaynor, whose support he appreciated most of all. The second officer recalled Borrik's advice about the security chief—that he wasn't "as big an idiot as he appeared." Apparently, the Dedderac's assessment had been an accurate one.

When it came to performing his duty, Gaynor seemed to put his personal likes and dislikes aside. Kirk was glad. It was hard enough to command a vessel without having to watch one's back at the same time.

The second officer thought for a moment. Then he made his decision. "Lieutenant Lynch and Lieutenant Jankowski," he said, "gather whatever equipment you need and report to the transporter room."

The science officer absorbed the information with equanimity. "Aye, sir," he told Kirk.

"Acknowledged," Jankowski responded.

Next, Kirk turned to the security chief. "When they're ready," he told Gaynor, "we'll batter down what's left of the satellite's shields. Then we'll effect the transport."

The man didn't say anything in response. He just nodded.

"I guess I'll head back to sickbay, then," said Velasquez, "and hope my services aren't needed any time soon."

"Permission granted," said the second officer. He took in the others at a glance. "Any questions?"

There weren't any.

"All right," he said. "Then let's move."

* * *

Mitchell watched the forward viewscreen, where the damaged alien satellite was looming larger and larger as the *Constitution* bore down on it. *Here we go,* he thought.

"We're in range!" he called out.

"Fire!" Kirk commanded.

As Gaynor worked his controls, two bloodred phaser beams lanced across space and raked their target. Mitchell could almost feel the satellite shuddering under the assault.

But a second later, the *Constitution* paid for her audacity. The other two visible satellites launched a counterattack, filling the screen with blue-white fury.

The deck shivered and the navigator was forced to hang on to his console to keep from being thrown out of his seat. Sparks erupted from one of the unmanned control panels near the turbolift.

"Damage report!" Kirk demanded.

"Shields down seventy-eight percent!" Mitchell responded. "Damage to decks three and four!"

"What about the satellite?" asked the second officer.

"Its shields are almost gone," Borrik told him. "One more volley and it will be defenseless."

Kirk looked encouraged. "Fire again, Mr. Gaynor!"

"Aye, sir," bellowed the security officer.

Once again, the *Constitution* stabbed at the satellite with twin beams of destruction. This time, her target rolled under the impact, its shields disabled and perhaps several other systems as well.

The communications officer's voice resounded with triumph. "Its shields are down, sir."

Before Mitchell or anyone else could react to the news, the viewscreen blanched with the ferocity of the satellites' response. The *Constitution* groaned and lurched under the force of the barrage, making him feel like a rodeo rider trying desperately to hang on to his bronco. Then, just for good measure, another perimeter station exploded, exposing them all to a cascade of hot, white sparks.

"Shields down ninety-one percent!" the navigator cried. Dark, acrid smoke began to gather above the ruined console. "Damage to decks seven and eleven!"

"Transporter room is ready!" Borrik added.

Mitchell saw the muscles work furiously in his friend's jaw as he leaned forward toward the viewscreen. Despite the tense nature of their circumstances, despite the lives hanging in the balance, Kirk seemed sharper and more focused than ever before.

My god, the navigator thought. *The instructors at the Academy were right. He really was born to command.*

"Drop shields!" cried the second officer.

"Dropping shields!" Mitchell replied, his fingers crawling urgently over his controls.

Down in the transporter room, the technician on duty was taking note of the move and beaming Lynch and Jankowski across the void to the disabled satellite. Unfortunately, that would take a couple of seconds—and during that span, the *Constitution* would be utterly vulnerable.

The navigator stared at the screen, bracing himself for another white-hot burst of energy from the surviving satellites. *Come on,* he thought, his teeth grinding together. *Come on.*

After what seemed like an eternity, he heard Borrik's voice again. "They're on the satellite!"

"Shields up!" Kirk ordered. "Evasive maneuvers!"

Just then, Mitchell saw another blinding-white barrage blossom on the screen. For a moment, it seemed it would hammer the *Constitution* just as hard as its predecessors had. Then it seemed to stop growing, as if it were losing its enthusiasm for the task.

But the navigator knew that wasn't happening— not really. Actually, they were withdrawing from the wounded satellite as quickly as they could, racing farther and farther away from the source of the energy beams in the hope that when they hit, they would do so with less intensity.

"Impact in two point six seconds!" Gaynor roared.

The navigator cursed beneath his breath and held on to his console again. A heartbeat later, the bridge shivered and lurched under the influence of the satellites' energy blasts.

Still, Mitchell decided, it wasn't as bad as it could have been—as bad as it surely would have been if they hadn't tried to distance themselves from the satellites. Despite the flimsy state of their shields, ship and crew had managed to survive the bombardment.

And Lynch and Jankowski had been safely deposited on the disabled satellite. The navigator grunted with satisfaction. All was proceeding according to Borrik's plan.

He turned to look at Kirk again. The second officer

noticed and returned the look. *So far, so good,* he seemed to say.

Darick Lynch had always considered the transporter process the greatest marvel of his age. The present instance was no exception.

One moment, he was standing on the *Constitution*'s transporter platform with Chief Engineer Jankowski beside him, both of them sporting black shoulder bags full of equipment. The next moment, they found themselves bathed in a sickly green light, surrounded by a small, pentagon-shaped room with a high ceiling and an array of computer workstations that appeared to cover every square millimeter of wall space.

"Pay dirt," said the engineer, smiling and moving eagerly to the nearest control panel.

Lynch took out his communicator, flipped it open, and raised the device to his mouth. "We're in," he reported back to the *Constitution,* "and we're proceeding as planned."

"Acknowledged, Lieutenant," came the transporter technician's brief and efficient reply.

By then, Jankowski had taken out her tricorder and established a link with the alien computer system. Moving quickly, the science officer stowed his communicator and took out a portable transmitter. Then he stood it on its tripod and linked it to the engineer's tricorder as well.

"Ready?" she asked.

"Ready," said Lynch.

Her fingers stinging the tricorder keys, Jankowski

got the download process started. "There," she told her companion with an air of satisfaction. "Now all we have to do—"

Before she could get another word out, she was stabbed in the side by a series of slender, white energy pulses. They made her jump like a puppet on a string, her head lolling back and then forward again. Even before the engineer slumped to the deck, her body giving off wisps of black smoke, the science officer knew she was dead.

Worse, Jankowski had hit the transmitter when she fell, knocking the thing offline and terminating the datalink. And worse still, the energy pulses continued to shoot across the space between them, preventing Lynch from reaching over to correct the situation.

A backup system, he told himself. *Of course.* He had to let Kirk and the others know he had run into trouble.

Taking his communicator out of his shoulder bag, he flipped it open and said, "Lynch to *Constitution.* Come in, *Constitution.*"

But there was no reponse. The science officer cursed out loud. For all he knew, the station's deflector shields had come back up and his signal hadn't even gotten through.

He reached into his shoulder bag and pulled out his tricorder this time. Then he played it all around him. It showed him a force shield surrounding a good deal of the satellite—its heart, no doubt.

It wasn't a very strong field, however—not like a deflector, by any means. It might scramble a voice signal or a transporter beam, but not a high-integrity data transmission. And it wouldn't prevent Lynch from leaving the room via its single door and contacting the *Constitution* from another part of the station.

If he did that, he reflected, he could get out of there in one piece. He could survive to tell everyone what had happened.

But that wasn't his mission, was it? The science officer glanced at his colleague, who was lying on the deck with her mouth gaping and her dead eyes staring at the ceiling.

"No," he said out loud, answering his own silent question. It wasn't at all what he and Jankowski had come here to accomplish.

Lynch forced himself to look at the bright flashes of energy that still traversed the space between him and the engineer. It seemed to him they didn't cover the entire area, the way a true energy barrier would, though it was difficult to tell because the pulses were intermittent.

Biting his lip, he considered the idea of just sticking his hand out at the right time and trying to right the overturned transmitter. But that wouldn't accomplish anything, really; the science officer needed to restore the datalink as well.

Besides, if his timing was off, he would absorb a pulse. He didn't know if just one would be enough to kill or even disable him, but he couldn't take the chance with so much riding on his efforts.

No, Lynch decided calmly. He wouldn't just reach out and depend on his sense of timing. He would track the pulses on his tricorder and try to judge the distance between them. And if there was enough space there, he would take the next step.

It took what seemed like a long time for his tricorder to do the job. Finally, however, it showed the science officer what he needed to know. The interval between the height of one pulse and the next was almost seven and a half inches.

It was more than he would have guessed from observing the phenomenon with the naked eye. Substantially more, in fact.

Lynch looked at his arm, which couldn't have been more than five or six inches in diameter at its widest point. If he could slip it between the lowest pulse and the floor, he might be able to reach the transmitter, restore the link, and retract it unscathed.

Of course, if he slipped more than an inch or so in either direction, he would run the risk of ending up like Jankowski. It was a chilling thought—but not so chilling that it deterred him.

To increase his chances of success, Lynch stripped off his uniform shirt, exposing his bare skin. After all, he didn't want to lose his life because of a stray piece of sleeve. Then he took a breath, dropped to the floor, and reached tentatively in the direction of the transmitter.

It couldn't have been more than two feet away, though it seemed like twice that. With the pulses sizzling past his eyes, ever more blinding as he edged nearer to them, the science officer extended his hand along the deck as far as it would go.

Fortunately, it was just far enough. The pulses shot by so close to Lynch that he could feel their destructive heat on his skin. Still, he was able to wrap his fingers around one tripod leg of the transmitter and pull the device back a few inches.

That was all the leeway he needed. First, he stood the thing up again. Then he reprogrammed it to speak with Jankowski's tricorder, which was lying on the deck beside her.

A moment later, the science officer saw a light go on, indicating that the transmitter was doing its job again. He breathed a sigh of relief. Then slowly, carefully, Lynch pulled his arm back along the deck and retreated from the pulse field.

You did it, he told himself, leaning against the bulkhead behind him. *You got it going.*

Unless there was some other obstacle he wasn't aware of, the *Constitution* would be receiving the station's data again immediately. And with it, Lynch's fellow officers would figure out a way to pull the Sordinians' bacon out of the proverbial fire.

Lynch looked at Jankowski, whose skin was taking on a waxy look in death. *If only you were still alive to see it,* he thought sadly. *If only you knew you hadn't died for nothing.*

Chapter Eleven

KIRK DRUMMED on the armrest of the captain's chair with his fingertips, trying to be patient.

He would much rather have beamed over to the alien station with Lynch and Jankowski. However, the landing party couldn't have been a large one, and it was clear they were more qualified than he was to handle any technical problems that cropped up.

"Mr. Kirk," said Borrik.

The second officer turned in his seat and saw the Dederrac's worried expression. "What is it?" he asked.

"The dataflow has stopped," Borrik reported.

"Stopped?" Kirk echoed. He cursed softly. "Contact the landing party, Lieutenant. Ask them what's going on."

A moment passed as the communications officer

worked. Then another moment, and another, and Borrik's expression kept souring.

The second officer got up and made his way to the Dedderac's console. "Lieutenant?" he prodded.

"I cannot get through to them," Borrik rasped. "Something is getting in the way of my signal."

His control panel beeped as if with annoyance.

Kirk turned to the viewscreen, where the alien station could be seen in the distance. It didn't look operational, but . . .

"Have its deflectors gone back up?" he wondered out loud.

"No, sir," Gary responded smartly, his gaze moving from monitor to monitor. "Deflectors are still down."

"Whatever has happened," the Dedderac pointed out, "the effect is not comprehensive." He continued to scan the data coming in through the sensor net. "Part of the satellite is still open to communications—but it's not the part Lynch and Jankowski beamed onto."

The second officer felt a trickle of icewater in the small of his back. Clearly, something had gone wrong on the satellite. He needed to find out what it was.

"Wait," said Borrik. He turned to Kirk, his features pinched with puzzlement. "We're receiving data again."

The second officer glanced at the communications console. Sure enough, it was flashing one ruby-red graphic after another.

"And voice communications?" he asked hopefully.

The Dederrac shook his head. "No, sir. Those are still blocked."

Kirk grunted. Had something happened to the landing party's communicators . . . or to the landing party itself? He turned to Gary. "Scan for life signs, Mr. Mitchell."

"Aye, sir," said his friend. After a second or two, he looked up from his controls with an expression of dismay on his face. "I seem to be reading only one set of signs."

No, the second officer thought. *It can't be.*

Not another one.

For a fraction of a second, he felt as if he were on the bridge of the *Republic* again, surrounded by death in every direction. Then, mercifully, the feeling passed.

"Which one is it?" Kirk asked numbly. "Lynch or Jankowski?"

Gary worked some more, then gave up. "I can't tell, sir. There's something in the way of my scan—probably the same thing that's blocking Mr. Borrik's comm signal."

The second officer gritted his teeth. There was no fooling himself—he had a situation on his hands. One of his officers was dead and the other one . . . who knew what kind of condition he or she might be in?

"Sir," said Medina, his voice sharp with urgency, "we seem to have another problem. An unidentified vessel is approaching us at full impulse. Heading two four oh mark six."

Kirk swallowed. "On screen."

The alien station vanished from the viewscreen. In its place, the second officer saw a daunting sight—a dark, powerful-looking ship with four large, egg-shaped nacelles. Unless Medina had seriously screwed up the magnification factor, the thing was ten times the size of the *Constitution*.

It also bore a marked resemblance to the orbital stations. As if to underline the fact, the helmsman spoke up again.

"Sensors show she draws on the same technologies as the satellites." Medina glanced over his shoulder at Kirk. "It appears they were manufactured by the same people, sir."

The second officer looked at the screen again. The alien vessel was bristling with arcane-looking armaments from stem to stern. Clearly, the *Constitution* was no match for her when it came to firepower.

"The mother ship," Gaynor spat.

"Jankowski was right," Borrik added.

The orbital stations had just been a warm-up, Kirk realized, a taste of things to come. This was the featured act, he thought as he returned to his center seat.

"Estimated time of arrival?" he asked, despite the uncomfortable dryness in his mouth.

"Four minutes and twenty seconds," came Medina's reply.

Gaynor turned to him. "We've got to get out of here, sir."

Instinctively, Kirk shook his head. "Not without our survivor, Lieutenant, whoever it is."

The security chief's mouth became a thin, hard line. "Lynch and Jankowski would understand the need for us to withdraw, sir."

The second officer regarded him, locking eyes and wills with the man. "We're not leaving," he insisted.

Gaynor's nostrils flared. "If we don't leave, sir, everything they've done could be for nothing. At least take a moment to go over the data. Maybe it'll show us something useful."

"By then," Kirk pointed out, "Lynch and Jankowski will both be dead. That's not acceptable."

The security chief turned red in the face. "Not acceptable . . . ?" he sputtered. "What about the destruction of the ship and the rest of the crew? Is that acceptable, Lieutenant?"

The second officer didn't so much as flinch. "You're out of line," he told Gaynor with a confidence he didn't feel. "Way out of line."

The older man continued to glare at him. But as angry as he was, Gaynor stifled any further acts of rebellion. Swearing beneath his breath, he turned back to his security console.

That battle fought, Kirk reflected on the matter at hand. He had less than four minutes until the alien mother ship arrived—less than four minutes to figure out a plan of action and pursue it.

He sensed that everyone on the bridge was staring at him. Gary. Medina. Borrik. And Gaynor—him, most of all. As the ship's engines pulsed like a secret heart, they waited to see what their acting commander would do.

He knew what he wouldn't do. He wouldn't leave

his surviving comrade behind to die or be captured by the aliens.

"All right," the second officer said, his mind racing ahead of him, "here's what we're going to do." He turned to the security chief. "We're going to send two of your officers over to the satellite, Mr. Gaynor. They'll reconnoiter, see if they can help either Lynch or Jankowski. If they can, fine. If they can't, we'll beam them back."

Even as he described his plan, he knew how difficult it would be for him to beam those officers back empty-handed. It went hard against his grain to abandon even one of his people—and not solely because of the horrors he had seen on the *Farragut*.

It was simple, really. He just couldn't help imagining himself as the one being abandoned.

Gaynor considered Kirk's order, giving no indication of whether he would carry it out or not. Then the security chief tapped the intercom stud on his black control console.

"This is Gaynor," he said, "calling officers Zuleta and Park. Meet me in the transporter room." He glanced at Kirk. "And bring your phasers, boys. I've got a mission for you."

Kirk nodded approvingly. "Thank you, Lieutenant."

"Don't mention it, sir," the chief replied with a hint of irony in his voice. "I'm just following orders, you know?" Then he left the bridge by way of the turbolift.

The second officer watched as the doors hissed shut behind Gaynor. Then he turned to the forward viewscreen again, where the alien ship was looming larger and larger by the second, and prayed fervently that he had made the right decision after all.

It seemed to Lynch he had barely left the alien data center behind when he heard the faint, metallic echo of footfalls.

Damn, he thought. *There wasn't supposed to be any life on this station. We were supposed to be alone when we beamed over.* His hand moved in the direction of his phaser.

Then it occurred to him that the footfalls might not have come from the enemy. After all, Kirk had lost voice communications with the landing party when the aliens' backup system kicked in. He might very well have beamed over a rescue squad.

Yes, the science officer told himself, reaching for his tricorder instead of his weapon. *A rescue squad. That's it.*

A moment later, his tricorder confirmed it. Two life-forms, both human. They were farther away than Lynch had estimated, but he would see them coming from the other direction in just a few seconds.

Then they could all go back to the *Constitution,* their mission accomplished. And sometime later, when the threat of the satellites had been disabled, they would return for Jankowski's body.

The science officer fixed a picture of the woman in his mind, recalling her warmth and her ready smile. *Don't worry,* he told Jankowski. *I may be leaving without you, but I won't let you stay here for long. And neither will your friend Hirota.*

He sighed. The first officer would be anguished when he heard about Jankowski. He wouldn't show it—Lynch was certain of that. But in private, the man would bawl his eyes out.

Who wouldn't? the science officer thought. It was harder than hell to lose a woman with whom you had fallen in love. Unfortunately, Lynch knew that from his own experience.

He consulted his tricorder again. The rescue team was definitely getting closer. What's more, they had probably registered the science officer's approach the same way he had registered theirs.

It couldn't hurt to call out to them. That way, there wouldn't be any mistakes. "Hello," he shouted, his voice echoing resoundingly from bulkhead to bulkhead. "It's Lynch."

"Lynch," came the reply, echoing just as resoundingly. "It's Park and Zuleta. Are you all right?"

The science officer scowled, reminded of his partner's fate. *"I* am," he called back. "Jankowski's dead."

Just as he said that, he saw the two security officers come around a corner up ahead. They had both phasers and tricorders out, and there was a distinct look of urgency on their faces.

"It's all right," Lynch assured them. "We're alone here."

"We've got to hurry," said Zuleta, looking past the science officer just in case. "Are you sure Jankowski's dead?"

"Positive," Lynch replied, as he let Park grab his

arm and pull him along the corridor. "But why the hurry? What's going on?"

The security officers told him. The aliens' mother ship had been detected and it was headed for the *Constitution,* but Kirk had insisted on getting his team off the satellite before he withdrew.

Part of Lynch was grateful for the second officer's loyalty and generosity. But the other part of him couldn't help cursing the man because—in Lynch's opinion, at least—he had made the wrong damned choice.

"Mr. Kirk?" said Borrik.

The second officer turned to him. "Zuleta and Park made it over?" he asked, hoping for confirmation.

"They did indeed, sir," said the communications officer.

Kirk nodded and said, "Acknowledged, Mr. Borrik." Then he returned his attention to the forward viewscreen and the alien juggernaut steadily bearing down on them.

With the least bit of luck, the security officers they had sent over to the satellite would find Jankowski or Lynch—whichever one still lived—and bring him or her to an interference-free site before too much more time expired. Then they would all beam back to the *Constitution,* and the ship would make her retreat in one piece.

The second officer heard the turbolift doors hiss open. Before they could close again, he saw Gaynor return to his post at the security console. The security chief cast a glance in Kirk's direction, but didn't comment further on the younger man's decision.

After all, the dice had been cast. Now it was just a question of how they would come up—lucky seven or snake eyes.

"They're powering up their weapons," Gary reported suddenly.

Kirk clenched his jaw. Without any shields to speak of, the *Constitution* wouldn't be able to withstand much of an attack—and the mother ship looked more dangerous than all the satellites combined.

But the second officer wasn't leaving. He had already made that decision. He was going to stick around as long as he could to give his landing party a fighting chance.

Kirk was about to call for evasive maneuvers when the alien vessel released a quick burst of dark blue fury. *Don't tell me they're firing on us already?* he thought.

The second officer saw the enemy ship release a second burst and a third in quick succession. But it didn't make sense to him. At this range, he told himself, the *Constitution*'s weapons couldn't have done any real damage to the alien. Was it possible the aggressor's weapons were that much more powerful than their own?

Then Kirk realized he was wrong about the mother ship's target. The vessel wasn't firing at the *Constitution* at all. It was firing at the damaged satellite, of all things.

The first splash of purple fire seemed to envelop the alien artifact, to set it burning like a torch in the darkness of space. Then the second ball of flame pierced the satellite to its heart like a fatal shaft. A moment later, the satellite exploded in an expanding frenzy of blue-white light, blotting out the stars for a moment and sending shards of dark debris spinning wildly in every direction.

Even after the light receded and died, fragments of alien material and alien technology continued to whirl haphazardly through the void. Some of them seemed on the verge of smashing into the *Constitution*, though that was just a trick of magnification.

But the rest of it was no trick. The second officer could see that with his own eyes. It was all too real.

No, Kirk screamed in the recesses of his mind, recoiling as if he had been lashed with a white hot whip. *No . . .*

"They blew up the satellite," Medina said in a dazed way, giving voice to the others' horror. "Maybe to . . ." He shrugged. ". . . to keep us from getting our hands on it, maybe?"

It was as good an explanation as any, the second officer thought. But he felt numb, sluggish, as if he were using someone else's brain.

Gary turned to him, his expression one of sadness and loss. "Your orders, sir?" he asked.

My orders, thought Kirk. *I have to give orders. Lynch and Jankowski are dead. Park and Zuleta are dead. Captain Garrovick is dead, too. But I'm alive and so are all these people around me, and they need me to get them out of this mess.*

He eyed the alien vessel, looming in the distance, looking for all the world as if it were eyeing him back.

As yet, the mother ship hadn't come after the *Constitution*.

"Withdraw," he said. "Full impulse."

"Aye, sir," Medina replied, bringing the vessel about.

"Now you withdraw?" asked Gaynor.

The second officer looked at him. The man had left his station and was standing at the bridge's red-orange rail, glowering at him.

"Now," he said, "when it's too late? When you've lost not only Lynch and Jankowski, but Zuleta and Park into the bargain?"

"That's enough," Kirk told him.

"No," Gaynor went on, his hands gripping the rail so hard his knuckles turned white, "it's not enough. It's not nearly enough. If not for you, those people would still be alive, dammit! They'd still be alive!"

The second officer felt his cheeks heat up. Under different circumstances, he would have thrown a man in the brig for comments like those. But he didn't, and for a very good reason.

He wasn't certain that Gaynor wasn't right.

"I did what I thought best," Kirk replied evenly. "And as long as I'm in command of this ship, I'll continue to do what I think best." He met the security's chief hot, angry gaze. "Is that understood?"

For a second or two, it wouldn't have surprised the second officer if Gaynor had leaped over the rail and gone for his throat. But as it turned out, the man did nothing of the sort.

Maybe he remembered then that the ship was still in the grip of an alert. Maybe it occurred to him that

Kirk had let him go farther than any other commander would have. Or maybe he just figured he couldn't do anything for his men anymore anyway.

Whatever the reason, Gaynor seemed to cool down, to get a grip on himself again. Then the man relinquished his hold on the rail and replied, "Yes, sir. It's understood, all right."

"Good," said the second officer. He turned to Gary. "Are they offering pursuit, Mr. Mitchell?"

The navigator solicited some computations from his console. After scanning them, he shook his head. "It doesn't look that way, sir. The mother ship is slowing down."

Kirk got up and eyed the viewscreen. Sure enough, the alien vessel was beginning to diminish in size as the *Constitution* sped away. Apparently, its captain had no desire to go after them.

But that didn't do Sordinia IV any good. With their defenses battered, the natives wouldn't last very long against the aggressor. Perhaps a few hours, at most.

Then the second officer remembered. "Mr. Borrik, the data from the satellite . . . how much of it did we manage to get?"

The Dedderac checked his monitor. "Quite a bit," he answered. "Possibly all of it. It is difficult to say."

Kirk nodded. At least he had bought something with the crewmen he had sacrificed like so many poker chips . . . as if that could make the horror any easier to take.

"What about the captain?" he asked Borrik, hoping against hope that the interference in the planet's atmosphere had cleared.

The communications officer shook his black-and-white striped head. "I have attempted to contact him periodically, as you requested, but I have yet to meet with any success."

The second officer frowned. "Keep trying, Lieutenant."

"Aye, sir," said the Dedderac.

Kirk stared at the viewscreen. He had never felt more miserable in his life—not even that awful night on the *Farragut*. He needed time to think, to sort things out.

"Mr. Borrik," he told the communications officer, "send the data Lynch and Jankowski collected to the briefing room."

"As you wish, sir," the Dedderac responded.

The second officer turned to Gaynor. "You've got the conn," he said. "I'll be back after I've reviewed the data."

The security chief scowled at him. "Acknowledged."

Without another word, Kirk made his way to the turbolift. After what seemed like a long time, the doors opened and he got inside. When they finally closed behind him, he pounded the heel of his fist on the wall—not once, but three times, each blow harder than the one before it.

What have I done? he thought, as he cradled his fist in his other hand. *What have I done?*

Chapter Twelve

KIRK PULLED A CHAIR OUT from the briefing room table, sat down and reached for the controls in the base of the three-sided monitor unit. Manipulating them, he saw the monitor screens come to life.

Each screen showed the same solid block of data, reflecting the merest portion of whatever information had been in the satellite's computers. It would be up to the second officer to cull through it and find something he could use against the enemy.

Certainly, Kirk could have assigned the task to one of his subordinates. He could have given it to Borrik or Gary or even Gaynor and no one would ever have called him on it.

But he was the command-track officer in the group. He was the one who had been trained to see things others might have missed and to turn them into significant advantages. And he was the one to whom Captain Augenthaler had entrusted his ship and crew.

Under the circumstances, he couldn't let someone else go through the data. He had to do it himself.

But as he began to pore over it, he thought again of Lynch and Jankowski. And of Park and Zuleta. And of the decisions he had made that had sent them all to their deaths.

Was Gaynor right? he wondered. Had he done the wrong thing by not sacrificing the survivor of the first landing party?

It wouldn't be the first time he had hesitated and watched his colleagues die as a result. Once before, he had been called on to make an important choice and chosen badly.

No, he told himself. *I can't think about this. I have to find a way to beat the mother ship, and I have to find it now.*

Suddenly, Borrik's voice came crackling over the intercom system. "Lieutenant Kirk?" said the Dedderac.

"I'm here," the second officer responded. "What is it?"

"The aliens' barrage has stopped," Borrik reported.

"Stopped?" Kirk echoed. He sat back in his chair. "Just like that?"

"If I were to speculate," said the Dedderac, "I would say it had something to do with the arrival of the mother ship. It is the only discernible event that has taken place in the last few minutes."

The second officer considered the possibility.

"Whatever the reason," he decided, "we have to assume it's only a respite. Have you tried to contact the capitol again?"

"I have, sir," Borrik responded. "However, even with the barrage discontinued, the atmosphere is still too highly charged for me to get a signal through. We can only hope that will change."

Kirk nodded. "Thank you, Lieutenant."

"Borrik out," came the dutiful reply.

The second officer eyed the data on the three-sided monitor. He still couldn't relax, he told himself. Not when the attack on the capital might resume at any moment.

However, he could get a cup of coffee.

Kirk got up, went to the food unit in the room and punched in his requirements. The unit beeped and produced a mug of steaming black coffee.

He returned to the table and set the mug down on the dark, polished surface. Then he took his seat again, stole a sip of the coffee and returned his attention to the monitor.

But before he could really dig in, he was interrupted again—and this time, it wasn't by unwelcome thoughts *or* Mr. Borrik. It was the door mechanism, chiming to tell him that there was someone outside requesting entry.

Normally, of course, someone could just walk into the briefing room unannounced. But Kirk had set the mechanism to screen prospective visitors in an attempt to concentrate on his work.

Sighing, the second officer got up and touched the control pad set into the bulkhead. As the doors slid aside, they revealed his friend Gary standing outside in the corridor.

Kirk looked at him. "Aren't you . . ."

"Supposed to be on the bridge?" the navigator asked. "I was. Then my shift ended and my replacement arrived."

That's right, thought the second officer. *Gary's shift would be ending about now.* "And you decided to give me a hand?"

His friend shrugged. "You looked like you needed help . . . of some kind. I'm here to give it to you, whatever it is."

Kirk looked at him. "Come on in," he said.

Gary entered and took a seat beside the second officer's. Then he glanced at the monitor. "You're still at the beginning," he observed.

The second officer nodded. "It was difficult to concentrate."

"You had things on your mind," his friend suggested.

Kirk grunted. "Things."

For a moment, neither of them spoke, the steam from Kirk's coffee curling in the air between them. Then Gary asked, "Do you want to talk about it? Or are you determined to wallow in your misery?"

The second officer felt a hot spurt of anger in his throat. It was easy for his friend to make the problem sound trivial. After all, he wasn't the one who failed his captain so miserably. He wasn't the one with two hundred deaths on his head.

He wasn't the one who had to live with all those ghosts.

"You look angry," Gary told him.

"It's none of your business how I look," Kirk responded. He took a sip of his coffee and put it down again.

The navigator ignored the remark. "That's good," he said. "You're getting angry. Maybe I can make you even angrier. Maybe you'll get so furious you'll finally tell me what's eating away at you."

For a moment or two, the second officer was tempted to tell Gary to go to hell. But he didn't—and he realized why. He wanted to unburden himself as much as his friend wanted to take on that burden.

"All right," he answered. "You asked for it."

Gary sat back in his chair. "I'm all ears."

Kirk frowned. "You asked me the other day if something happened on the *Farragut*—something that had me down. Well, something happened, all right. Something pretty bad."

His friend didn't say anything. He just sat there, listening. And after all, wasn't that what the second officer wanted him to do?

Taking a deep breath, Kirk launched into his story. "As you know, I spent the last three years serving on the *Farragut* under Captain Garrovick."

The navigator nodded. "Uh-huh."

"I was never assigned the same duty two days in a row," the second officer recalled. "Garrovick told me it had to be that way if I was going to command a starship of my own one day. He said a captain had to know every last little detail of his vessel, every one of its strengths and weaknesses—not to mention the strengths and weaknesses of his crew."

"You mentioned that in one of your subspace communications," said Gary. "Just before I was posted to the *Constitution,* I think."

"And did I tell you where I spent most of my time?" Kirk asked.

The navigator shrugged. "At the helm, I'd imagine."

"Sometimes," the second officer agreed. "But I wound up in engineering a lot, too. And also at the forward phaser station."

Gary grunted softly. "Somehow, it's hard for me to picture a fast-tracker like you at a phaser station."

Kirk shook his head. "Captain Garrovick didn't seem to have a problem picturing it. I was there two, maybe three times a week. But nothing ever happened. All I ever saw there were a lot of stars rushing past."

"I know the feeling," the junior officer remarked.

"Then we came to a world called Tycho Four," said the second officer. "It was a small, red planet scored with deep fissures and pocked with dormant volcanoes—but rich as hell in dilithium ore. Captain Garrovick kept us in orbit for a day and a half, sending down teams on a rotating basis to take readings and samples. Naturally, I was on the planet's surface every chance I got."

After all, to a young officer, the worst duty planetside was preferable to the best job back on the ship. People joined Starfleet to see alien landscapes, not the inside of a duranium hull.

"But just before we were supposed to leave," Kirk continued, "the first officer sent me to the forward phaser station. I got over there, exchanged pleasantries with the ensign I was replacing, and sat down. Then I ran a quick diagnostic. Everything checked out fine, so I locked my hands behind my head and leaned back in my chair."

He paused, feeling his heart start to pump harder, feeling the muscles spasm in his jaw.

"And?" his friend prodded.

"And that's when I saw it," the second officer said, remembering the moment. "In the distance."

Gary eyed him. "Saw what?"

Kirk winced, perceiving the thing on his phaser-station monitor all over again. He was fascinated by the memory, unable to put it aside.

"Something big and white and gaseous," he breathed, "translucent in some spots and too dense to see through in others. It was rolling toward the ship like a storm-driven cumulus cloud."

The navigator didn't seem to understand. "I thought you told me you were above the planet's atmosphere."

"We were," the second officer said. "It only looked like a cloud. As it turned out, it was something quite different."

He felt his heart sink in his chest. "I stood there for a second, maybe two," Kirk related. "I was entranced by the thing. After all, I had never laid eyes on anything likc it." He swallowed, still locked into his recollection. "And the way it advanced on us, hesitating and then surging ahead, hesitating and then surging . . . I got the feeling that it was alive."

Gary looked at him. "Alive?"

The second officer nodded. "As alive as you or I, except in a different form. Where we're flesh and blood, it was made of something else—its molecules more loosely arranged."

The navigator shook his head. "Hard to imagine."

"But there it was," said Kirk, "hovering in front of me. Finally, I remembered where I was and what I was doing there, and I forced myself to stop gaping at the thing. My hand went to the phaser firing panel and locked on to the creature's coordinates, just in case it turned out to be a threat."

Just in case, he added silently, appalled now at his naïveté. If only he had known then what he knew now.

"Mind you," he declared, "I didn't think it *would* be a threat. I was just acting in accordance with Starfleet procedures. Then, without warning, the thing vanished from my external sensor monitors."

Gary's eyes narrowed. "It was gone?"

Kirk shook his head. "Not gone."

"Then where was it?" his friend asked.

"I didn't know at first," said the second officer. He shivered, remembering. "Then I felt something brush past me."

Suddenly, he had an urge to get up, to move. He left his seat and his coffee mug and circumnavigated the table.

"It was like a breeze," he said, "but too cold to be a breeze . . . horribly and ineffably cold. And I smelled a strange, sickly-sweet odor in the air, as I were being smothered in molasses." His nostrils flared. "It was

194

the thing . . . the cloud. It had gotten into the *Farragut* somehow."

Gary looked skeptical. "But, Jim, if it got into the ship, that would mean it was—"

"Intelligent," Kirk responded. "I know." He stopped and sat down on the edge of the table. "I could feel it as I lost consciousness." The sensation came back to him with terrible intensity. "A predatory alien mind, thinking . . . planning . . ."

"Are you sure?" asked the navigator.

The second officer nodded solemnly. "As sure as I can possibly be," he said softly.

For a heartbeat, he fell silent. The only sound in the briefing room was that of the engines. Then Kirk went on with his story.

"When I came to," he said, "I found myself lying in the corridor outside the phaser station. I must have staggered out there at some point, though I had no recollection of it. There were others there, too. Lots of them, in fact. And . . ."

The second officer felt a lump in his throat, keeping him from finishing his sentence. However, he believed Gary could divine what he was trying to say from his expression.

"They were . . . dead?" his friend asked.

"Dead," Kirk declared, finding the strength to say it at last. "Cold and white and rigid as marble statues, drained of every last red corpuscle in their bodies."

The navigator's brow creased with comprehension. "And you think the cloud thing did it?"

Kirk nodded. "I knew it even before I checked the

sensor records. The creature had made its way through the corridors of the *Farragut,* hunting down crewmen and feeding on their blood. And when its hunger was satisfied, it had gone back out into space."

Gary's eyes narrowed. "The sensor records confirmed that?"

"They confirmed it, all right. Down to the last grisly detail," the second officer told him.

Gary shook his head. "It must have been horrible."

"More horrible than you can imagine."

"I'm sorry, Jim. Really."

"Not half as sorry as I am," Kirk responded. He got up and came around the table again. "After all, I'm the one who killed them."

It took his friend a moment to understand what he was talking about, but Gary finally got it. And when he did, he balked at the logic that had led the second officer to that conclusion.

"No," the navigator insisted. "That's wrong. You said you only hesitated for a second or two."

Kirk smiled bitterly. "A second or two . . . in which I might have destroyed the thing with a maximum-intensity phaser barrage—and preserved the lives of more than two hundred men and women, the captain included."

"You don't know that," his friend argued.

"I know those people are dead," the second officer countered, "and I know I didn't do anything to protect them. I know I just sat there, spellbound by the sight of an unfamiliar life-form, failing to discharge the responsibility entrusted to me by my captain."

Gary looked puzzled. "But your commendation—"

"Was an empty one," Kirk told him, dismissing it with a gesture. "After it was over, after the creature was gone, I went up to the bridge and gave some orders. Got us moving again, that sort of thing. But truthfully, I should have been court-martialed instead of commended."

He sat down heavily and drew a deep, painful breath. "So now you know," he told the other man. "Now you know everything."

Mitchell regarded his friend. Kirk's eyes seemed to have taken on a harder cast. Shadows had collected beneath them. Clearly, telling his tale had taken its toll on him.

But, finally, the navigator had the whole hideous picture in front of him. And at last, he believed he understood.

Ever since that day on the *Farragut*, Kirk had been racked with sadness, with guilt and uncertainty. He had walked among the spectres of the *Farragut* dead, apologizing to them for his failure each step of the way.

It was no wonder the second officer had seemed distant when he arrived on the *Constitution*. It was no surprise he hadn't warmed to any of his colleagues— not even his old Academy buddy.

In a dark corner of his mind, the man was still reliving that pivotal moment when he could have pressed a pad and unleashed a phaser barrage at the cloud creature. He was still replaying the memory and punishing himself when he hesitated, the way he had in life.

Then, suddenly, it had become more than a memory. Kirk had been thrust into the command chair of the *Constitution* and forced to make a life-and-death decision. And once again, his hesitation—albeit of a different variety—had resulted in a tragic loss of life.

"Jim," said Mitchell, "the life of a Starfleet officer is full of tough decisions. I don't have to tell you that. But we all do the best we can . . . and afterward, we move on."

The second officer gazed at him with tortured eyes. "I can't move on, dammit. Don't you see? I waited too long to help those people on the *Farragut*. And then, just a little while ago, I waited too long again— and four of my fellow officers paid the price."

The navigator nodded, seeing exactly what his friend was talking about. "And now you're afraid you're going to do the same thing over and over again. You're afraid that when the next crisis materializes, you're going to make another mistake and cost someone his or her life."

Kirk sighed. "I don't want anyone else to die on my watch, Gary. I've got enough ghosts to last me a lifetime . . . and then some."

Mitchell drew a breath, then expelled it. *All right, then,* he thought. *I tried to skirt the issue, but my pal doesn't want to do that. So we'll go the other way— we'll confront it head-on.*

"Listen, Jim," he said, "I don't know what happened on the *Farragut* that day, and I don't think anyone, alive or dead, is in a position to judge you on that count. But when it came to Jankowski and Lynch and what took place on that satellite . . ."

His friend looked up at him. "Yes?"

The navigator frowned. "I think you made the wrong decision. I think you should have gotten the *Constitution* the hell out of there, landing party or no landing party."

Kirk regarded him. "So you agree with Gaynor?"

"I do," Mitchell told him.

His friend didn't argue his case. He didn't say anything at all. He just sat there and absorbed the comment.

"But you won't make the wrong decision next time," the navigator said. "Or the time after that."

"How do you know that?" Kirk asked, his voice hostile and full of resentment. "One of your flashes of insight, I suppose?"

Mitchell smiled. "I don't need them in this case. You're Jim Kirk, remember? You're the guy they say is the most promising young officer on the block. Do you think Starfleet Command put you on the fast track these last several years because they like the way you part your hair?"

The second officer sighed. "It's one thing to have the tools . . . and another to be able to use them."

"You know how to use them," Mitchell assured him. "Hell, you've been using them since you were in your teens. You can't let a couple of tragedies strip you of your confidence, Jim. You're a good officer, a fine officer. You just need to keep telling yourself that, ghosts or no ghosts."

Kirk eyed him. No doubt he was thinking that his

friend's advice was something easier said than done. But at the same time, he seemed to draw hope from what the navigator had told him.

At last, the second officer nodded. "All right," he said. "I'll keep telling myself that."

"Good," Mitchell told him. He turned to the monitor in the center of the table. "Now, where were we?"

"At the beginning," Kirk reminded him.

"That's right," the navigator remarked. "And I was going to give you a hand, wasn't I?"

The second officer smiled a wary but grateful smile. "I believe you were," he agreed.

Together, they went over the data on the monitor. After a while, however, they decided they weren't progressing quickly enough—so they split up the task, each of them using one of the monitor's three sides. And they didn't even think about stopping until Lieutenant Borrik's voice invaded the briefing room more than half an hour later.

"Mr. Kirk," said the Dedderac, "the attack on the capital has resumed. And this time, the alien vessel has joined in."

Mitchell cursed beneath his breath, picturing the kind of devastation the mother ship could rain on the capital. "That doesn't give us much time. We've got to pull something out of this database before—"

He stopped, realizing his friend wasn't listening to him. He was staring at his side of the monitor as if entranced.

"Jim?" he said.

"Mr. Kirk?" Borrik joined in, no doubt confused as

to why he wasn't getting a response from the second officer.

Just then, Kirk looked up. "I've got it," he said.

"Got what?" Mitchell asked.

"A way to stop the aliens," his friend explained.

That got the navigator's interest. "What is it?"

The second officer glanced at the ceiling. "Mr. Borrik, I want you down here on the double. The same goes for Mr. Gaynor and Dr. Velasquez. Also, Polcovich and Banks."

"Aye, sir," said the Dedderac.

Burning with curiosity, Mitchell gazed at Kirk. "Dammit, Jim, are you going to tell me what you found or aren't you?"

When his friend looked back at him, he seemed a lot more confident than he had a half hour earlier—a lot more secure. It seemed, at least in Kirk's opinion, that he had really discovered something valuable.

"All in due time, Lieutenant," the second officer replied thoughtfully. "All in due time."

Chapter Thirteen

KIRK LOOKED AROUND the briefing-room table. Gary was there, of course. So were Gaynor, Velasquez, and Borrik, just as he had requested.

In addition, there were two other faces at the table. One belonged to Polcovich, a tall, fair-haired woman who had reported to Lynch. The other belonged to Livingstone, a squarish, heavy-browed fellow who had served under Jankowski in engineering.

Though Kirk had gotten rid of the cup, the place still smelled of cold coffee. And one other thing, he thought. Anticipation.

"We don't have much time," said the second officer, "so I'll try to be concise. As you're all aware, the situation has changed. Initially, all we had to deal with were the alien satellites."

"But not anymore," Gaynor remarked impatiently. "Now we've got the mother ship to worry about, too."

"Exactly right," Kirk told him, resisting the urge to bow to the man and proceed too quickly. He walked around the table, speaking as he went. "But part of what made the satellites so formidable was that they were able to act in a decentralized fashion, without any one station guiding the actions of the others. The system is centralized now, which, in a way, makes it more vulnerable."

Gary nodded, obviously beginning to see where his friend was going with his remarks. "Because if you can take out the mother ship, the threat represented by the satellites will be nullified as well."

"Right again," the second officer confirmed. "The problem is we can't take out the mother ship—not with all those satellites working in concert with her. And we can't take out the satellites until we take out the ship."

"The chicken and the egg," said Livingstone.

Kirk scanned the faces in the briefing room. "The chicken and the egg, all right. But there may be a way to incapacitate the whole network, leaving the chicken alone to fend for herself."

"How do you propose to do that, sir?" asked Polcovich.

The second officer turned to her. "I'm going to batter down a section of the mother ship's shielding and send a team over—not for the sake of reconnaissance, but to sabotage the mother ship's ability to communicate with the satellite stations."

He let his words sink in for a moment. As he could have predicted, Gaynor didn't look happy about them.

"Batter down the shields and transport a team over. Sounds familiar," observed the security chief.

"Begging your pardon, sir," Livingstone interjected, putting an even finer point on the comment, "but isn't that the same approach that got Lieutenant Lynch and the others killed?"

That was the question Kirk had been waiting for. The one he knew he would have to face sooner or later.

"It's similar," he conceded. "But Starfleet officers have been beaming onto enemy facilities for a long time, Mr. Livingstone. They're not going to stop because of a few casualties, no matter how tragic."

Livinstone didn't push the matter. No one else did either.

"May I assume, sir," asked Borrik, "that you have located the enemy's communications center?"

"I have," said the second officer. "It was in the data we downloaded."

"And a way to disable it?" Livingstone inquired.

"That was in there, too," Kirk told him.

"What if the aliens have a backup communications system?" asked Polcovich. "That's a possibility, isn't it?"

"It's more than a possibility," said the second officer. "It's a fact. According to the data our landing party gathered, the aliens back up almost every operating system they have. My guess is that's the problem Lynch and Jankowski ran into."

Gary grunted. "How long before backup communications cuts in?"

"Anywhere from fifty seconds to five minutes after we disable the primary system," Kirk replied. "It'll take that long for the system to recognize the problem and come online."

"So that's our window of opportunity," the navigator noted.

"Indeed it is," Kirk confirmed. He stood up again. "We've got that long before the mother ship regains control over the satellites. Which means we've got to destroy her in that window—or not at all."

There was silence around the table. The second officer chose to look at that as a positive development.

"And what about the landing party?" Velasquez asked at last.

"When the aliens can no longer control their satellites," Kirk told her, "we'll beam the landing party back—and take our chances with the mother ship one on one."

Polcovich regarded him. "Begging your pardon, sir . . . but do you think we'll have a chance against her?"

"I do," the second officer responded. "Judging from the information we downloaded, the aliens clearly have the advantage when it comes to firepower—but not when it comes to maneuverability. Their propulsion technology can't hold a candle to ours."

The Polcovich mulled her superior's conclusion. "Let me know if there's anything I can do to enhance that edge," she said.

"I will," Kirk promised her.

Gaynor rolled his eyes.

The second officer regarded him unflinchingly. "Was there something you wanted to contribute, Chief?"

Gaynor straightened. "I was just wondering," he said. "When the time comes, are you going to have the guts to destroy the enemy? Are you going to blow up that ship without a second thought?"

Kirk had thought about that, too. "I'm not particularly looking forward to it," he answered frankly and without rancor. "But if it's a matter of saving the Sordinians, I'll do it."

"Get off his back, Jack, " Velasquez told Gaynor, her voice the lash of a whip. She glanced at the second officer. "I have faith in Mr. Kirk, even if you don't."

The security chief chuckled humorlessly. "I'm not the only one who's lost faith in him, Doctor." But he didn't get more specific than that.

"I'm sorry to hear that anyone's lost faith in me," the second officer told them all. Then he turned to Gaynor. "But I'm not here to please you or anyone else, Mister. I'm here to do a job."

The muscles worked in the chief's jaw. Still, the man didn't say anything in return.

Kirk scanned the faces of the others. "I'll need five volunteers," he said simply. "Not only from those of you in this room, but from the security and engineering sections as well."

"I'll go," Gary told him, raising his hand.

"I would like to go, too," said Borrik.

Then a third hand went up. To the second officer's surprise, it belonged to Chief Gaynor.

"Count me in," said the chief.

Kirk didn't understand. Gaynor had expressed a lack of confidence in the second officer. And yet he seemed willing to put his life on the line for the man's plan.

Kirk was reminded again of the way Borrik had described the security chief outside the lounge. *Jack Gaynor is a proud man. A professional.*

Despite his personal opinions, Gaynor knew that his commanding officer had set him a task. Like Kirk, he had a job to do. And he was going to do it, come hell, high water, or cosmic anomalies.

A moment later, Polcovich volunteered as well. So did Velasquez. Only Livingstone remained silent, obviously less than enamored with what he saw as Kirk's prospects of success.

Nonetheless, the second officer had the landing party he had wanted. Or most of it, at least.

"Mr. Mitchell," he said, "will remain here on the *Constitution*. Likewise, Lieutenant Velasquez."

Gary looked at him, disappointed. The doctor, too.

But Kirk couldn't let either of them go. If they were going to tackle the aggressors' mother ship, he needed his best navigator on the bridge. And as for Velasquez . . . eager as the doctor was, she didn't have the skills that would be needed by the landing party.

The second officer turned to Gaynor. "You'll be the officer in charge. Borrik and Polcovich will follow your lead. And you'll bring along two other security officers as well—your choice."

It was Kirk's way of recognizing the chief's sense of responsibility. His way of saying that, no matter what had happened between the two of them, Kirk was a professional as well.

The chief nodded. "Acknowledged, sir."

"Report to the transporter room in five minutes," Kirk added.

"Aye, sir," came the measured response.

The second officer looked around the table—both at those of his people who would be going and those who would be staying behind. Silently, he wished he were with the first group.

"Dismissed," he told them.

Standing in the turbolift, listening to its motors shrill, Mitchell glanced at his friend Jim. "I would dearly have loved to be part of that landing party," he said.

The second officer nodded. "I know. But I needed you here with me. Medina is a terrific helmsman, but he doesn't have much experience working on the bridge of a Constitution-class starship."

"And I've got several years' worth," the navigator conceded.

"Exactly," said Kirk. "You know the old saw . . . never put a neophyte at the forward console if you've got a veteran available. And in this case, Lieutenant, you're available."

Mitchell grunted. "I guess I am."

The second officer frowned. "Besides," he admitted, "I like the idea of having you around."

The junior officer turned to his friend and smiled. "Thanks. I'll try not to disappoint you."

A moment later, the lift doors opened, exposing them to the buzz and hustle of the bridge. Emerging from the lift, Kirk took the dark empty center seat. At the same time, Mitchell moved to the helm-navigation console, where a dark-haired crewman named Masefield had taken over for him.

Noting the primary navigator's approach, Masefield yielded the post to him and returned to the weapons station. With a nod to recognize the man's efforts, Mitchell sat down behind the console and diligently began checking his operations monitors.

Warp and impulse drives were online and functional, he saw. Sensors, both active and passive, were working at full capacity. The same for the ship's communication and weapons systems, transporters and life support. Even the ship's shields had been brought up to full strength with power borrowed from less critical areas, and repairs had been made to those decks that had suffered in the exchange with the satellites.

They seemed to be in good shape. But then, the navigator told himself, they would have to be. Depositing a team of saboteurs on the aggressors' mother ship wouldn't be an easy feat to pull off.

"Mr. Wooten," said Kirk, addressing the communications officer who had taken over for Borrik, "let me know when Chief Gaynor and his team arrive in the transporter room."

"Aye, sir," answered Wooten, a square-jawed man with a head of thick, curly red hair.

Then the second officer turned to the viewscreen.

Mitchell turned to it, too, taking stock of the alien vessel depicted on it. It was firing twin energy beams at the planet's surface.

Before, the aggressor ship had seemed impressive in its capacity for destruction. Now that they were set on confronting it, Mitchell thought, it looked even more so.

We're taking a chance here, the navigator told himself. *We couldn't even match up with the satellites. Throw in the mother ship and we may really be out of our league.*

But there was a planet full of people depending on them for help. They couldn't ignore that fact. If they failed, Mitchell mused, it wouldn't be for lack of trying.

"Mr. Kirk," Wooten announced, "I have word from the transporter room. The team is ready."

The second officer nodded. "Thank you, Lieutenant."

"Aye, sir," came the reply.

Mitchell watched Kirk sit back in his captain's chair and gather himself. Then he said, "Listen carefully," and explained to his bridge personnel the plan he had unveiled in the briefing room.

When he was finished, he asked if there were any questions. There weren't any. If anyone had any misgivings about the second officer's scheme, he had decided to keep them to himself.

"Very well," said Kirk. He took in his crew at a glance. "Report to battle stations. Raise shields, Mr. Mitchell. Mr. Masefield, power up the weapons array."

Instantly, the bridge became a flurry of activity. Critical stations were activated and manned. And in the middle of it, the navigator erected the ship's newly restored deflectors. In a matter of seconds, the *Constitution* was ready to go into combat.

The second officer turned his gaze on Lieutenant Medina. "Take us in, helm. Three-quarters impulse."

"Aye, sir," said Medina, carrying out the order.

Before Mitchell knew it, they were bearing down on the aggressors' ship, targeting whatever weak points Masefield might have discovered in her shield architecture. The navigator bit his lip, wondering how the enemy would respond to their approach.

As it turned out, he didn't respond at all. His sensors must have showed him the *Constitution*'s flight pattern and the status of her weapons batteries. Still, the alien vessel just sat there and continued to fire at the capital, as if her commander weren't the least bit concerned.

It wasn't a promising sight, the navigator remarked inwardly. The aliens were either very stupid or very confident. He was afraid it would turn out to be the latter.

"Range," Masefield reported.

Mitchell couldn't turn around to see the look on his friend's face, but he could hear the tone of Kirk's voice. There was nothing tentative about it anymore. It had the hard certainty of duranium in it.

"Fire phaser beams!" commanded the second officer.

Twin shafts of phased energy sliced through the black of space, spearing the alien ship. The navigator thought he saw the aggressor shudder with the impact, but it was difficult to be sure.

"Direct hit!" Masefield noted.

"Her shields are starting to buckle!" added Medina.

It was true. They had made some progress. Mitchell could see it all on his red and black tactical monitor.

But before Kirk could give the order to unleash another barrage, the enemy returned fire, filling the viewscreen with a wave of crackling, white fury. They could have tried to elude it—except it wasn't just the mother ship that was firing back at them, but the satellites as well.

Mitchell felt the deck pitch and tremble and make noises like someone in pain. But he couldn't do anything about it. All he could do was hold on to his console and ride out the storm.

Kirk's voice cut though the groaning of the bulkheads like a knife. "Report!" he ordered.

"Shields down thirty-two percent!" the navigator barked back.

"Damage to Decks Seven, Eight, and Ten!" Wooten announced.

The second officer considered the viewscreen, where the enemy vessel was looming larger and larger every second. "Fire again!" he called out. "Phasers and photon torpedoes!"

"Aye, sir!" cried Masefield.

As Mitchell looked on, the *Constitution* released a combination of red-orange phaser beams and bright yellow torpedoes. They traveled straight and true and found the mother ship.

This time, there was no mistaking it. The alien vessel was jarred by the *Constitution*'s assault.

"Direct hit again, sir!" the weapons officer told Kirk.

But, as before, the enemy wasn't taking the attack lying down. The navigator saw another surge of blinding-white chaos fill the viewscreen, the collaborative effort of both the enemy ship and its orbital satellites. He barely had time to grab his console again before it tried to jerk its way out of his grasp.

Along the perimeter of the bridge, the engineering station exploded, showering the crew with white-hot sparks and sending a plume of black smoke into the air. Fortunately, the station had been unoccupied at the time, or its operator would certainly have been killed in the blast.

This time, the second officer didn't have to call for reports. They came to him freely, without his asking.

"Shields down fifty-eight percent!" Masefield bellowed.

"Damage to Decks Thirteen and Fourteen!" Wooten chimed in.

"But we're getting somewhere," Mitchell observed, ignoring the harsh, acrid stench of the smoke. He consulted the sensor data pouring into his monitors, one crimson graphic after another. "One more strike like the last one and we'll have a hole big enough for a transport."

"Good," said Kirk. He glanced at Masefield. "Fire again, Lieutenant—and this time, give it everything you've got!"

"Aye, sir!" the weapons officer called back.

Masefield took the second officer at his word. This time, four fully loaded photon torpedoes accompanied the *Constitution*'s phaser beams as they stabbed at the steadily nearing mother ship.

The result was evident on Mitchell's monitors. The bombardment had opened a gap in the enemy's shields, just as he had predicted. He spun in his seat to face Kirk.

"Now!" he cried out.

The second officer tapped a stud in his armrest. "Energize!" he told the ship's transporter technician, who had been waiting for the order in the transporter room on Deck Seven.

Just then, the aggressor vessel and its satellites retaliated—and at closer quarters than before, their power was even more devastating. The navigator attempted to take hold of his console again, but he might as well not have bothered. Before he could anchor himself, before he could do anything at all, the deck seemed to spin about beneath him and whip him savagely out of his chair.

Mitchell had the feeling that he was flying. Then something smashed him in the ribs, sending shoots of pain through his chest and knocking the wind out of him.

As he gasped for air, darkness playing at the edges of his vision, he felt a pair of hands grab him and pull him to his feet. Looking up, he saw that they belonged to his friend Jim.

"Are you all right?" Kirk asked, blood oozing from an angry cut over his left eye, black smoke billowing behind him.

Even as he pulled in fire-seared air to fill his lungs again, Mitchell nodded. He couldn't speak yet, but he did his best to assure the second officer that he was still fit for duty—that he was still Kirk's best bet when it came to the navigation console.

After all, the junior officer thought, he had come this far. He wasn't about to let himself get dragged off the bridge now, when things were just starting to heat up.

The second officer turned to Medina, who was just crawling back into his seat. "Evasive maneuvers!" he commanded. "But make sure to stay well within transporter range!"

"Aye, sir!" the helmsman shot back.

Turning to the viewscreen, Mitchell saw the mother ship fire again and braced himself. But as the energy assault blossomed in their direction, it began to slide toward the edge of the screen. The closer it got, the faster it slid—until finally, it left their sight altogether.

Inwardly, Mitchell rejoiced. They had eluded the aggressors' beams, thanks to Medina's deft piloting. But the helmsman would need help if he was going to keep on eluding them.

The navigator pushed his friend away and returned to his post. "I'm fine," he rasped as he plunked himself down in his seat, anticipating a repeat of Kirk's question.

The second officer frowned, but accepted Mitchell's claim as the truth. "What's our situation?" he asked.

The navigator took a look at his monitors. "Shields are down eighty-eight percent," he reported. "Nineteen casualties, but none fatal. Damage to nearly half the decks on the ship. However, all operating systems appear to have remained intact."

Thank heavens for that, at least, Mitchell thought. But what about the landing party? Had they made the transport despite the last attack?

A moment later, Kirk turned to Wooten and asked that very question. The communications officer, who had been listening to an open intercom channel, smiled with a bloodied mouth.

"They made it, sir," said Wooten. "Chief Gaynor and the others are on the alien ship."

The second officer didn't wait to be told twice. Turning to Medina, he said, "Get us out of here, Lieutenant."

The helmsman didn't need any further encouragement. Executing a gut-wrenching turn, he brought the *Constitution* about. Then he sent them retreating at full impulse, lighter by five crewmen.

At the same time, the alien juggernaut left the viewscreen. After all, the screen had been programmed to scan the area ahead of the starship.

Kirk glanced over his shoulder at Wooten. "Rear view!" he demanded of the communications officer.

A moment later, the mother ship swung back into the center of the screen. But from its diminishing image, Mitchell could tell it wasn't offering pursuit. It was circling back to join its satellites.

And why not? the junior officer wondered. As far as the alien vessel's commander was concerned, he had beaten off the Sordinians' only discernible defender.

The battle for the planet was over and, from all appearances, the invaders had won.

But then, he didn't know yet that Kirk had deposited a squad of saboteurs on his ship. And by the time he discovered what had happened, it would be too late for him to stop them.

At least, that was the plan.

The navigator saw that his friend was looking at the screen as well. By then, the flesh around his cut had begun darkening into a nasty bruise. Kirk turned to Wooten again. "Assign repair teams to all damaged decks," he ordered the communications officer.

Wooten nodded. "Aye, sir."

Finally, the second officer looked to Mitchell. They had done it, he seemed to say. The rest was up to Gaynor.

The navigator took a deep breath, let it out. Waiting, he thought. It was by far the worst part of the job. More than ever, he wished Kirk had made him part of the landing party.

Chapter Fourteen

GAYNOR LOOKED AROUND and saw he was no longer on a Starfleet transporter platform, his phaser in one hand and his tricorder in the other. He was standing in a narrow, high-ceilinged corridor near a metal door, bathed in an eerie green light.

And he was alone.

For the space of a heartbeat, he had the feeling it would remain that way. Then Borrik materialized on one side of him and Polcovich materialized on the other. And a moment later, they were joined by Chafin and Reboulet, the security guards he had chosen to accompany him.

There must have been some trouble with the transport, Gaynor concluded. *Interference from the energy bombardments or something. We're lucky we all arrived in one piece.*

Using gestures alone, because he didn't know if his voice might set off some kind of internal sensor alarm, he positioned Chafin and Reboulet at either end of the corridor. Then, glancing at the others, he indicated the door behind them.

On the other side of it was the ship's communications center. They knew that from the alien data they had downloaded from the satellite, which had conveniently included information on any number of things—ship schematics among them.

If they could disable the communications center, the aggressors' entire cybernetic system would become useless. The vessel would lose its ability to coordinate with its satellites.

For a short time, anyway. What was the estimate Kirk had given them? Anywhere from fifty seconds to five minutes. And then a backup system would cut in, rendering whatever the team had accomplished there null and void.

If they had had more time, Gaynor might have tried to decipher the pad set into the bulkhead beside the door. As it was, he simply raised his phaser and blasted the thing with an angry, orange-red beam. The pad sparked for a moment, then went dead.

By then, Polcovich and Borrik were tugging at the door, trying their best to slide it open. The security chief put his phaser and his tricorder down and gave them a hand. After a second or two, he felt the panel budge. Then, as if they had snapped some kind of lock, the door slid free and unhindered into a slot in the bulkhead.

Recovering his tricorder and his weapon, Gaynor

got up and peered inside. The communications center was empty. It was also quite small—barely big enough for three of them to occupy at once—which was why they hadn't beamed into it in the first place.

It had the same high ceiling and the same pale green illumination the chief had seen outside. But the bulkheads weren't smooth—far from it, in fact. The place was lousy with raised circuitry, all of which seemed to radiate from a half-dozen rounded nodes.

Taking a couple of steps inside, Gaynor used his tricorder to confirm that the nodes were tiny power cells—boosters that allowed the ship to speak with the satellites over long distances. So far, their intelligence was right on the money.

At this range, the mother ship couldn't have needed more than one of the cells to communicate. But without at least one, she couldn't send a message around the corner—which was was why Gaynor and his team would make sure to disable *all* the cells.

The tricky part would be up to Borrik and Polcovich. If they did their job right, the backup system wouldn't be triggered until they took out the last cell—and when the clock started ticking, there would be ample time for Kirk to beam the landing party off and destroy the mother ship.

"All right," the chief whispered to the science officer and the Dedderac, "let's get started." Pointing his weapon at the ceiling, he stood aside so they could enter the comm center.

But they had barely gotten inside before he heard the sound of footsteps from down the corridor. For a moment, they all froze. Then Gaynor gestured for Borrik and Polcovich to start working.

As they followed his order, he put away his tricorder and moved to the entrance. Then he peeked out into the corridor, where Reboulet was glancing anxiously at Chafin. As the chief established eye contact with the man, he saw Chafin point to the junction of passageways up ahead of him.

He had heard the footfalls, too, he was saying. And they were coming from the direction he was indicating.

As Gaynor listened, he could hear the sounds getting louder. And closer—there was no mistaking it. He scowled. This wasn't good, he told himself. This wasn't good at all.

It was possible that this was a single alien on some routine errand. But it was also possible that they had tripped some internal sensor alarm despite their caution.

If he was right, their mission was in grave jeopardy. Once the aliens confirmed that there were intruders aboard, they would activate their backup comm system manually—and that window of opportunity Kirk had counted on would never open.

Chafin held his hands out and shrugged, seeking guidance from his superior. The chief gestured for him to hold his ground and be patient. After all, they needed time, and there was no sense engaging in a confrontation sooner than they had to.

Then Gaynor turned to Reboulet, who was awaiting his orders as well. He was tempted to move her to Chafin's side to give the man some support, but he thought better of it. After all, an alien might approach them from the other direction next.

Poking his head back into the communications center, the chief saw that Borrik and Polcovich had pried the cover off one of the power cells and were starting to work on it.

Hurry, Gaynor urged his colleagues with silent intensity. *You may not have much time.*

Ensconced in the captain's chair, his forehead throbbing around the cut he had suffered in his fall, Kirk glared at the image of the aggressor vessel on the bridge's forward viewscreen. The aliens were still battering the capital with their powerful energy beams, looking as if they would be content to do so for the rest of eternity.

And there was nothing he could do about it. Or, to look at it another way, he had already done everything he could. He had sent over Gaynor and the others to even the odds.

Let's go, the second officer urged them. *Let's get the job done so I can bring you back home.* Every second that the landing party remained on the mother ship felt like another stone piled on his neck and shoulders, weighing him down with guilt and uncertainty.

What if he had made the wrong choice again? he wondered. What if Gaynor's team had already been detected? What if they had been caught and killed for their audacity?

Not having received the aliens' entire database, he couldn't be sure the vessel didn't have an internal sensor network capable of identifying intruders. But even if there was no such network, the odds of the team going unnoticed on the mother ship got worse and worse with each additional minute they spent there.

No, Kirk told himself. *I'm not going to think that way. I'm going to maintain a positive outlook. I sent a squad of highly trained people over to that ship. They'll succeed because they have to.*

Behind him, the turbolift doors opened with a hiss, admitting Dr. Velasquez in a white lab coat. The woman was all business.

"All right," she said to everyone on the bridge, "I've got plenty to do in sickbay, thanks to your shenanigans, so let's save some time. I can scan you all with my tricorder, or you can simply tell me how you feel. If you're hurt, say so. If you're not sure, let me know that too. And if you're all right, just stay the hell out of my way."

Kirk turned to her and pointed to the wound over his eye. Frowning, the doctor approached him and ran her tricorder over it, then reached into her pocket. Producing a plastiskin seal, she applied it to the damaged area.

"That'll do for now," Velasquez judged. "Who else?"

No one said anything.

The doctor turned to the second officer. "Well?" she asked.

Kirk shrugged. "That's about it."

Velasquez grunted. "It'd better be. The way you folks drive this thing, I may not get a chance to make another house call."

She glanced at the viewscreen and the alien vessel for a moment, her eyes narrowing with apprehension. But she didn't linger there. After all, as she had said, she had plenty to do in sickbay.

With a last glance around the bridge, as if to make sure she hadn't missed anything, Velasquez turned and headed back to the turbolift. A few seconds later, the doors closed behind her and the woman was gone.

The distraction over, the second officer considered the screen again. "How much time?" he asked his navigator.

His friend Gary looked back at him. "Two minutes and twenty seconds, sir. By now, they ought to be pretty far along."

Kirk certainly hoped so. *Come on,* he encouraged the landing party, a silent cheerleader. *What in blazes are you waiting for? Give me the signal so I can beam you back.*

But there was no signal. Not yet, at least. There was only the subtle, almost imperceptible hum of the warp engines and the birdlike noises of his officers' control panels.

Kirk sighed and sat back in his chair, the most useless man on the bridge. All he could do was remain alert—so when Gaynor's team *did* establish contact, he could pull them out of there without a second's delay.

Maintaining his position at the threshold of the comm center, his phaser at the ready, Gaynor couldn't help studying the alien who lay stunned alongside the bulkhead behind Chafin.

He was a good seven feet tall, hairless and lean to the point of what would have been emaciation in a human being. He had skin the color and texture of parchment, and all he wore was a loose-fitting black garment gathered tightly at the waist.

As for the alien's countenance . . . it was long and gaunt with tiny black eyes, mere nostril slits for a nose, and an unpleasant gash of a mouth. Gaynor couldn't even begin to identify the oval prominences displayed on either side of its neck, but the sheer size of them seemed to indicate they served some important purpose.

It had been more than a minute, maybe as much as two, since Chafin had blasted the alien and dragged it to its present location. The fact that reinforcements hadn't arrived already told the chief that their visitor wasn't responding to an alarm when it ran into them. More than likely, it hadn't suspected a thing until it saw Chafin and got knocked off its feet by the man's phaser beam.

Gaynor looked in on Borrik and Polcovich, perhaps for the twentieth time since the pair had gone to work. By then, the Dedderac and the science officer had exposed all six of the comm center's power cells and were in the process of disabling their fourth. So far, the chief told himself, everything was proceeding according to plan.

Kirk's plan, he couldn't help thinking. Frankly, he didn't like the *Constitution*'s new second officer or anything about him, but he had to give credit where it was due.

Suddenly, Gaynor heard another set of footfalls.

His pulse accelerating, he craned his neck to look down the corridor.

Once again, Chafin was pointing. As before, the chief gestured for him to stay where he was. Then he repeated the gesture for Reboulet at the opposite end of the passageway.

Borrik and Polcovich had to be close to achieving their objective, he thought. If he and his security officers could hang on just a little longer, they would be all right.

He listened for the footfalls. They were getting closer, closer . . . and then something unexpected happened. The unconscious alien sprawled behind Chafin started to make a clicking noise.

For a fraction of a second, Gaynor thought the alien had shaken off Chafin's phaser stun and was waking up. Then he realized that wasn't the case at all. The clicking was coming from the oval nodes on either side of the unconscious alien's neck.

Why? the chief wondered. And more importantly, why now?

Could the nodes have been some kind of subcutaneous communications devices? And had they been activated because the alien hadn't been heard from in a while? To someone else, it might only have seemed like a possibility. But to Gaynor, whose instincts had been honed by twenty years of security experience, it was a dead certainty.

Suddenly, the footfalls stopped. Someone called out in a voice that sounded like the rustling of dry reeds—someone who must have heard the clicking and recognized that no one was responding to it.

It was a whole new ball game, Gaynor told himself. Whoever was trying to contact the unconscious alien might keep trying, allowing for the possibility that the problem was a mechanical one.

But the alien around the corner—the one who had stopped dead in his tracks—might not take the time to investigate. He might report the clicking to his superiors. And they, in turn, might realize that the failure to respond was taking place in the vicinity of their comm center.

We've got to move quickly, the security chief thought. *We've got to take him out before he can alert the others.*

Chafin must have followed the same logic, more or less, because he didn't wait for instructions—he just rounded the corner as quickly as he could and went after the alien. Gaynor didn't hesitate either. He followed on his officer's heels, just in case.

As it turned out, it was a good thing he did—because as the chief approached the corner, he saw Chafin go flying across the mouth of the corridor, propelled by a thin, silver-blue beam. Clenching his teeth, Gaynor dropped, rolled, and squeezed off a shot of his own.

Fortunately for him, the alien was lumbering full-tilt after Chafin, apparently oblivious of the possibility of other intruders. The chief caught his adversary square in the midsection, doubling him over and collapsing him into an awkward-looking heap.

Gaynor scanned the corridor for other aliens, but he neither heard nor saw any. Grateful for that, at least, he went to see about Chafin.

The man was still alive, but his right shoulder was a bloody ruin. More than likely, the chief decided, Chafin's collarbone had been shattered. And yet, despite the pain he had to be feeling, the officer still seemed to have his wits about him.

"Come on," said Gaynor, draping Chafin's good arm over his neck and lifting the man up, "we've got to get out of here."

"I'm with you, sir," the officer gasped dutifully, his face little more than a grimace.

Supporting Chafin's weight, the security chief hauled him back to the comm center and sat him down just inside the entrance. Borrik and Polcovich glanced sympathetically at Chafin, but didn't comment. They were too busy trying to disable the fifth of the six power cells.

"They'll be on us any second now," Gaynor told them. "And more importantly, they'll be warming up their backup system."

"Cutting down somewhat on our opportunity to destroy them," the Dedderac noted efficiently. "However, I believe there will still be an opportunity of some magnitude."

As he finished his sentence, the security chief saw a red light go out in the center of the naked power cell. Five down and one to go, he thought optimistically, as Borrik and Polcovich turned their attention to the last of the cells.

Then he heard the stamp of footsteps again. But this time, it was more than one set. It was several. And unless he was mistaken, the sound was coming from more than one direction.

Glancing at Reboulet, Gaynor saw that she was maintaining the position he had assigned her. But with the aliens approaching them from both ends of the corridor, it seemed more prudent to pull her back—and try to defend the operation from the cover of the comm center, cramped as it might be.

"Reboulet!" he barked. "Back here!"

As the woman responded to his command, the chief kept watch on the portion of the corridor that stretched in the other direction. He listened, as well. And what he heard wasn't encouraging.

As the aliens got closer, their approach sounded like a stampede. Gaynor couldn't even begin to guess at the numbers their commander was throwing at him. He began to wonder how long they could hold out.

Three minutes? Two? Maybe as few as one?

He glanced inside the comm center at Borrik and Polcovich. They were still working on the last power cell, sweat gathering in the creases of their necks, their very postures taut with urgency.

It didn't look good for the team's survival. And if Kirk had to take the time to beam them off the alien ship, it looked even worse for the outcome of their mission.

With these things in mind, Gaynor made a decision—a hard one, but the only conclusion he felt he could come to under the circumstances. As soon as the Dedderac and the science officer disabled the last power cell, he would advise Kirk to blow up the mother ship . . .

With the landing party aboard.

Holding on to his phaser with his right hand, the

chief reached for his communicator with his left and snapped it open. Then he peered out into the corridor, where he expected to see the aliens come charging around either corner at any moment.

"Let me know as soon as you're done," he told Borrik.

"I will," the communications officer assured him, his voice remarkably calm and even despite the tenseness of the situation.

Gaynor had worked with Borrik for a number of years. He wondered if the Dedderac had an inkling of what the chief was about to do. If so, he gave no indication of it.

Chafin groaned and his superior spared him a glance. *Hang in there,* Gaynor thought. *It'll all be over before long, pal—the pain and the uncertainty and everything else.*

The thunder of the aliens' approach was growing louder and louder. They would turn one corner or the other any second, the chief thought—maybe even both corners at once.

He suppressed a chuckle as he considered what kind of medal they would give him for this. In life, he hadn't been able to get Augenthaler to make him second officer. In death, they would probably make him a commander . . . for all the good it would do him.

Abruptly, Gaynor caught sight of the thing he had been waiting for—the vanguard of the aliens' rush. The first corner they came around was the one Chafin had been guarding, weapons in their hands and hissing sounds erupting from their long, pale throats.

The chief fired his phaser into the crowd, then pulled his head back to avoid a return barrage of blue fury. After a moment, he peered out into the corridor and fired again. Stationed just behind him, Reboulet was doing the same thing.

Together, they cut down three or four of the aliens—enough to make the rest of them think twice and retreat from the corridor. But no sooner had they withdrawn than another pack of them swung around the corner at the opposite end of the passageway.

As before, Gaynor and Reboulet unleashed red-orange beams into their midst. But there were more of them than in the last bunch and they didn't give up so easily. The security officers didn't have a chance to duck after each shot—they simply had to keep firing and take their chances.

Then the chief felt someone touch him on the shoulder and declare in his ear, with Dedderac precision, "That's it, Jack. We have disabled the final power cell."

About time, Gaynor thought.

Pulling his head in, he poked the button that activated his communicator, instantly establishing a channel to the bridge of the *Constitution.* "This is Chief Gaynor," he bellowed over the tumult.

"Kirk here," came the immediate reply.

The chief licked his lips, which had suddenly gone dry. His heart was beating like a hammer against his ribs as he spoke the words he had been contemplating: "You've got a sitting duck, Lieutenant. Blow her up while you've got the chance!"

"But what about—" the second officer began.

"Blow her up!" Gaynor bellowed, the tendons in his neck standing out like cables. "Do it now!"

A sitting duck, Kirk thought.

He eyed the forward viewscreen, where the alien vessel hung in space looking every bit as deadly and powerful as it had moments earlier. But according to Gaynor's advisory, it had been cut off from its satellites.

The aggressor ship was vulnerable all of a sudden, though it was impossible to say for how long that situation would prevail. If Kirk moved quickly enough, if he gave the appropriate command in time, he could destroy the vessel in his sights and put an end to the Sordinians' travails.

Of course, he would also be destroying Gaynor and Borrik and their team along with the aliens. He would be killing his own people to save billions of other beings.

The second officer prepared to give the order to fire. He began to do what he had failed to do on the *Farragut*—what he had failed to do on the *Constitution* as well, the last time he had had a landing party in jeopardy. He began to make the tough decision.

And then he stopped. Something inside him was stopping him from saying the words that would spell his people's doom.

The second officer cursed himself. *You've got to do it,* he thought. *You've got to make the tough decision, damn you, even if it means sacrificing a few lives. You've got to weigh the five of them against the welfare of an entire planetary population.*

But Kirk still couldn't bring himself to give the order. As much as he wanted to help the Sordinians, as much as he recognized the danger the aggressor vessel represented, he couldn't kill his own crewmen.

He just couldn't.

Gaynor was right, he mused bitterly. *You're not fit to command. When push comes to shove, you don't have the guts to run a starship.*

It stung the second officer to think that way. It hurt like hell. After all, he had devoted his life to becoming a Starfleet captain. He had trained for years to face this moment and others like it.

But still, he didn't open his mouth and give the order to annihilate the alien vessel. He was incapable of it, he realized, as long as there was even a slim chance of recovering his people.

Gary was staring at him. What's more, Kirk knew what the man was thinking. *Gaynor will die anyway, Jim—him and Borrik and the others. They'll die at the hands of the aliens. And they'll die cursing you, because now their deaths won't have meant anything.*

But the second officer wasn't about to let them die—not at the hands of the alien aggressors or anyone else. All he needed, he told himself, was a few seconds to get the *Constitution* back within transporter range.

Then Kirk could recover his people *and* blow away the aliens' mother ship, and the Sordinians would be safe as well. He could have his cake and eat it, too—and he would, he promised himself, he would . . . because he damn well wouldn't accept any other possibility.

"Take her in," he told Medina. "Transporter range."

The helmsman hesitated for a fraction of a second. Then he said, "Aye, sir," and manipulated his controls accordingly.

Gary gazed at him a little longer. Then, without comment, he turned back to his navigation board. But his feelings seemed clear nonetheless.

Ignoring them, the second officer tapped the communications stud on his armrest. "Transporter room, establish a lock on the landing party."

"Aye, Lieutenant," said the transporter technician, a man named Rawitzer, "but it could take a minute or two. Sensors show the team is no longer alone in the vicinity of the communications center."

"We haven't got a minute or two," Kirk informed him. "Get a lock on them now, dammit!"

"Aye, sir!" said Rawitzer.

"Kirk out," the second officer barked. He turned in his chair to face the helm again. "How much longer, Mr. Medina?"

"Fifteen seconds," the man told him.

Kirk glared at the viewscreen. The alien mother ship was beginning to wheel around in response to their hasty approach—and though they hadn't quite gotten within transporter range yet, they were almost certainly within range of the enemy's weapons.

"All available power to the shields," he called out. After all, they wouldn't have any use for their phasers until after they had recovered Gaynor and the others.

"Acknowledged, sir," said Gary, carrying out the second officer's orders with grim efficiency.

Kirk's hands were clenched into fists on his armrests, his teeth grinding so hard they hurt. After the beating the *Constitution* had taken at the hands of the aliens, he knew the ship wouldn't be able to take much more—maybe a couple of barrages at the outside. If his transporter technician couldn't get a fix on the landing party—and quickly—the second officer would have a lot more than five fatalities on his head.

He would have an entire ship's worth.

Chapter Fifteen

GAYNOR SQUEEZED OFF a shot at the aliens, then quickly pulled his head back into the communications center. A half-dozen light blue energy beams hit the bulkhead beside him a split second later, pounding the sleek, dark metal from two different directions.

Reboulet stuck her head out next and released a ruby-red phaser stream of her own. But as the aliens fired back and she tried to withdraw, one of their energy shafts struck her in the ankle. Unable to support herself, the security officer spilled awkwardly into the corridor.

Without thinking, Gaynor darted out from cover to grab his comrade and pull her back inside. But as soon as he exposed himself, the aliens unleashed another hellish crossfire.

Somehow, the security chief got his officer back inside. And somehow, he did it without getting smashed to pieces by the enemy's barrage. Then he looked at Reboulet and saw why. She had inadvertently served as a shield for him, absorbing so many shots to her left side that her uniform was drenched with blood.

Somehow, though, the woman had hung on to her phaser. Borrik took it from her and moved up beside Gaynor. The Dedderac's eyes told the security chief he wouldn't be any easier to discourage than Reboulet was.

But then, that came as no surprise. Gaynor knew what Borrik was made of.

But the man in charge of the *Constitution* was another story. Blast it, Gaynor raged as he fired another sizzling phaser beam at the aliens. What in blazes was Kirk's problem? Why was it taking the second officer so long to attack the enemy ship?

Kirk frowned as he watched the huge alien vessel bring its weapons ports to bear on the *Constitution*. "Mr. Medina?" he prodded hopefully.

"Just a moment more, sir . . ." the helmsman answered, watching his monitors. Then he announced, with a distinct note of triumph in his voice, "We're in range, Lieutenant!"

Charged with urgency, the second officer tapped the intercom stud in his armrest. "We're in transporter range, Mr. Rawitzer. Have you got a lock yet on the landing party?"

"Not yet, sir," came the reply.

"What's wrong?" Kirk asked, trying to control his impatience.

"I'm having trouble discerning our people from the aliens," the technician explained. "They're in close proximity now, and their bioprofiles aren't all that dissimilar."

The second officer considered the viewscreen, where the alien vessel was growing larger by the second. "Keep at it," he told Rawitzer, not knowing what else to say. "Kirk out."

It was just about then that the mother ship decided to unleash its considerable firepower. Its weapons ports belched blue-white fire at the *Constitution,* threatening to tear it apart.

But it was only the alien vessel that was firing, not its satellites. That made its directed-energy barrage a good deal easier to elude. As Medina pulled the starship hard to starboard, the second officer watched the blue-white blaze slide away from them on the viewscreen—leaving the *Constitution* and her crew unscathed.

Kirk leaned forward. "Return fire! Target engines and weapons batteries—phasers only!"

"Aye, sir!" Masefield called back.

A moment later, the ship's phaser beams jabbed at the enemy's vital parts. Unfortunately, they were unable to pierce the bigger vessel's defenses, though the attack went a long way toward weakening them.

The second officer would have liked to punch away at some other parts of the mother ship, some places where an energy strike might do more damage. However, he held himself in check.

The whole reason for this run was to rescue his landing party. It wouldn't make sense for him to do anything that might destroy the vessel before Gaynor and the others were recovered.

"They're coming back for another shot at us!" Gary reported.

"Rear view," said Kirk.

The image on the viewscreen changed. Once again, he found himself looking at the dark bulk of the aggressor ship as it came about and aimed its weapons ports. A moment later, the aliens unleashed another blue-white burst of destructive energy.

But as before, Medina was ready for them. This time, the helmsman brought the *Constitution*'s nose up sharply, allowing the enemy's barrage to pass harmlessly beneath them.

"Return fire!" the second officer called out. "Keep in mind the same parameters, Mr. Masefield!"

"Acknowledged, sir," the weapons officer responded.

As Kirk looked on, he saw his vessel's phaser beams test the mother ship's defenses again. And though the enemy's shields protected her, the assault rendered them even more fragile than before.

They were winning, the second officer told himself—and more important, they were buying the time they needed for Rawitzer to get a lock on the landing party. So far, the acting commander's decision looked like a good one.

Then it all changed.

His friend the navigator cried out that the enemy was powering up something new—some weapon they hadn't seen before. Before Kirk could respond, before he could even think about responding, he saw a blaze of yellow brilliance fill the viewscreen.

The next thing he knew, he was lying on the deck, the metallic taste of blood strong in his mouth. The engines were droning insistently at him; he could hear them in his bones.

Get up, they urged him. You've got to finish what you started.

Picking himself up, the second officer looked around to get his bearings. It was then he realized he was sprawled beside a peripheral station, outside the orange rail of the command center.

The other bridge officers had been wrenched from their seats as well, Kirk observed. A groaning Wooten was stretched out near the turbolift. Gary was sitting at the base of the center seat, shaking his head. And Masefield had been dumped unceremoniously in front of the viewscreen, where he was only now beginning to stir.

Only Medina seemed to be missing. Grabbing the rail and using it to pull himself up, the second officer looked around for his helmsman. Finally, he located him. Medina was lying facedown on the other side of the bridge, by the science station.

He wasn't moving a single muscle.

Kirk swallowed hard. *No,* he insisted. *I won't accept it. No more deaths, dammit. No more ghosts.*

Circumnavigating the rail, ignoring half a dozen painful bruises and worse, he made his way past Wooten and the turbolift. Then he got down on his knees beside Medina and checked the man's pulse.

It was still reasonably strong. But there was a trickle of blood from the helmsman's ear, signifying a head injury. He needed medical attention—and he needed it now.

The second officer turned to Wooten, who was only just then dragging himself back into his seat. "Contact sickbay," he told the communications officer. "Have Dr. Velasquez send a team up to get Medina."

"Aye, sir," said Wooten, and got to work.

Unfortunately, Kirk told himself, he couldn't linger alongside Medina. He had work to do. Making his way back along the rail, he regarded the viewscreen. The alien vessel depicted there was coming about— no doubt in preparation for another pass at them.

It didn't seem to be in any great hurry, though. Its commander probably believed he had taken the fight out of the *Constitution* with his crushing and unexpected assault.

And maybe he had, the second officer reflected. He had never seen a weapon like the one the enemy had brought to bear, nor had it been mentioned in the satellite's database. More than likely it was something new, something developed after the satellite was programmed.

Something Kirk hadn't taken into account when he made the decision to try to recover his landing party. And what had his oversight cost the *Constitution*? How bad a setback had it been?

"Report!" he called out.

"It was a muon burst," said Masefield, as he bent over his console to decipher the event. "At least, that's what the sensors say. But I've never seen anything like it."

Muons, Kirk thought. The aliens' weapons technology was even more advanced than he would have guessed.

By then, Gary had regained his seat as well. "Shields down ninety-two percent," he noted. His console trilled as he worked. "Damage to Decks Four, Six, Eight . . . almost everywhere. Repair teams have been dispatched." As he consulted his monitors further, he shook his head ruefully. "And the warp drive is offline."

"Casualties?" Kirk asked, dreading the answer.

"Plenty of them. But no deaths, apparently."

Kirk heaved a sigh. He was grateful for that, at least.

But . . . no warp drive? He considered that for a fraction of a second. In the short run, it might not hurt them, since the battle was currently being fought at impulse speeds. But in the long run . . .

He watched the enemy vessel face them, its weapons ports gaping wide with the promise of further devastation. It seemed to the second officer that they were in desperate need of a helmsman. Luckily, he knew just where he could find one.

Plunking himself down beside his friend, Kirk took control of the helm controls. Before the enemy could pummel them again with its secret weapon, he threw the *Constitution* into a pattern of evasive maneuvers.

It would be safer, of course, to retreat altogether—to make the hard decision that Gaynor and Gary both seemed to believe in. Certainly, no one would be able to argue with that course of action.

But he wasn't giving up on his landing party. *Not after I've come this far,* he resolved. *Not after I've risked so much. I'm going to hang in as long as I have to.*

He waited for the mother ship to fire at them, to rake them with its weapons. He waited for it to go after them.

But it didn't do either of those things. It just sat there as they twisted away, as it if knew they had to remain just inside the limits of transporter range.

"I don't get it," the second officer thought out loud. "Why aren't they trying to—?"

And then he saw the answer outlined in red on his helm monitors.

A moment later, Gary must have seen it, too, because he gave it a voice—and a relieved one, at that. "That monster blast depleted their energy supplies, Lieutenant. The enemy has barely got enough juice to keep his deflector shields up."

It was true, Kirk reflected. The aliens' sensor profile showed they were running on reserve power. They couldn't have attacked again if their lives had depended on it.

At least until their engines generated some more power—and there was no telling how long that might take. A minute, maybe? Several?

As the second officer pondered the question, he heard the turbolift doors whoosh open behind him. Glancing over his shoulder, he saw that it was Velasquez herself and one of her nurses with an antigravity stretcher, responding to his call for medical assistance.

"What was that?" the doctor asked as she helped lift Medina onto the stretcher. Her expression was one of disapproval. "We've got people down all over the ship."

"Lieutenant Kirk!" Wooten blurted suddenly. "I've gotten word from Rawitzer in the transporter room—he's got a lock on the landing party!"

As the doctor left the bridge with her latest patient, the second officer felt a new sprit of optimism. "Target the enemy, Mr. Masefield. I want to punch a hole in those shields."

"Aye, sir," said the weapons officer, fingers flying.

As before, he sent a stream of phaser fire at the mother ship's engines and weapons batteries. But this time, it wasn't a short burst. It was a prolonged assault on the vessel's defenses.

And in time, it had the desired effect.

"Their shields are down!" Gary cried out triumphantly.

Kirk saw it on his monitors. "Drop deflectors!" he commanded.

He knew the loss of her shields would leave the *Constitution* as helpless as the aggressor ship, but he also knew he had no choice in the matter. After all, this was the opening he had been waiting for.

As Gary complied with his order, the second officer punched in a channel to the transporter room. "Mr. Rawitzer," he snapped, "energize!"

The response was reassuringly crisp and instantaneous. "Aye, sir!" said the transporter technician.

As the comm link subsided, Kirk looked to the forward viewscreen again. To his naked eye, nothing looked any different. The alien vessel was still hanging in space, waiting for its weapons to recharge so it could reduce the starship to atoms.

But somewhere on board, there were a handful of *Constitution* crewmen—people who had risked their lives to disable the ship's connection to its satellites and succeeded—and if luck was with them, they were being whisked to safety at that very moment.

At least, that was the second officer's hope—and not just his, he knew, but that of his colleagues on the bridge and, indeed, that of everyone on the ship. They were all pulling for Gaynor and his team to make it back alive, to return to the *Constitution* the way they had left her.

Seconds passed, feeling more like hours. Kirk could feel the perspiration collecting in his hands and in the small of his back. Finally, he couldn't stand the waiting any longer.

He glanced in the direction of the communications station. "Did we get them?" the second officer asked.

Wooten didn't answer right away. He just pressed his headpiece to his ear and scrunched his features with concentration. Finally, he looked up and turned to face Kirk.

"Well?" asked the second officer, not at all certain he wanted to hear the man's answer.

"We got them, sir!" Wooten reported excitedly.

That was all Kirk needed to hear. Turning in his helmsman's seat, he faced the viewscreen and the dark aggressor ship depicted on it with a renewed sense of purpose.

"Shields up!" he barked.

"Shields up!" his navigator confirmed.

"Target the enemy!" he told his weapons officer.

"Targeted," said Masefield, his voice taut with anticipation.

The second officer glowered at the alien vessel, remembering how casually it had obliterated its own satellite with Lynch and Jankowski and his two security officers aboard. Four human beings—dead, just like that. It made what he had to do a little easier to contemplate.

"Sir," said Gary, "the enemy's shields are going back up!"

Kirk swore beneath his breath. Obviously, the aliens' power was coming back—and quickly. If he didn't end the battle now, the *Constitution* would eventually be exposed to another wave of destruction like the first one—and this time, it might not survive the encounter.

"They're powering up their weapons, sir!" called Masefield.

The second officer didn't wait to find out which ones. He called back, "Target phasers and photon torpedoes, Lieutenant—maximum intensity and full spread!" Then, as he gunned the impulse engines for a strafing run, he added, "Fire at will!"

The weapons officer did as he was told. As his fingers darted across his control panel, highly focused phaser emissions and yellow-white photon torpedoes erupted from all the *Constitution*'s weapons ports, scalding the fabric of space en route to their intended destination.

The phaser beams struck first, shredding the mother ship's returning shields and ripping a hole in her sleek, dark hull. Then the torpedoes plunged into the breach. For a moment, the second officer held his breath, wondering if there were some angle he had missed, some defensive system he hadn't counted on that would deny him his victory.

Then the enemy vessel exploded in a conflagration of staggering proportions, filling the viewscreen with a blinding, white light. Kirk brought his hand up to shade his eyes from the glare. When he brought it down again, there was nothing left of the aggressors' vessel except a few twisted pieces of debris spinning outward from the focus of the blast.

Gary cast a glance at his friend. "Direct hit, sir," he reported with a straight face.

Even then, still charged with the urgency of battle, the second officer couldn't help smiling a little at his navigator's remark. "I gathered as much," he replied.

Now all he had to worry about were the satellites. After all, they were still the same deadly threats they had been before the arrival of the alien vessel, ready to fire on either the *Constitution* or the planet's surface at the drop of a hat.

Kirk consulted his console about their status. At that point, the satellites still seemed quiet. It occurred to him that they might be awaiting orders from the mother ship.

Orders that would never come, he reflected. What's more, now that the alien vessel was out of the way, he believed he knew a way of dealing with the five remaining satellites—another product of the information they had downloaded from the first one.

"Mr. Wooten," the second officer said, "transmit the following code on a narrow beam to each of the line-of-sight satellites." Then he gave the communications officer the code in question.

Kirk waited until Wooten had a chance to do as he asked. Then he turned to his friend Gary again. "Mr. Mitchell?"

"Aye, sir?"

"Give me a view of the nearest satellite," the second officer instructed him. "Maximum magnification."

A moment later, the viewscreen filled with the by-then-familiar image of an alien satellite. The blue-green sweep of Sordinia IV's surface could be seen in the background.

Kirk eyed the satellite as if it were a living adversary. "What's its status now?" he asked the navigator.

Gary checked his monitors. When he answered the question, there was a note of surprise in his voice. "It seems to have shut itself down, sir. Weapon and shield functions are offline."

The second officer breathed a sigh of relief. Once again, the aliens' data had proven invaluable.

His friend looked at him askance. "Begging your pardon, Lieutenant, but if you could disable the satellites with a code . . ."

Kirk knew what he was getting at. "Why risk a

landing party to sever the satellites' link with the mother ship?"

Gary nodded. "That's what I was wondering, sir."

"Unfortunately," the second officer explained, "the code only works when the satellites are on their own. When there's a vessel overseeing them, it doesn't do a thing."

The navigator grunted. "I see," he said.

Kirk turned to his weapons officer. "Let's take it out, Mr. Masefield. Target and fire."

A few moments later, a single lurid phaser beam speared the satellite. What's more, it kept spearing it, until the thing exploded in a splash of fiery white light.

Kirk nodded his approval. Good riddance, he thought. But what he said was "Mr. Masefield, I'm going to bring us in range of the other satellites, one at a time. We have some loose ends to tie up."

"Aye, sir," the weapons officer responded with unconcealed eagerness.

Kirk understood the man's reaction too well. Neither Masefield nor anyone else on the bridge wanted to worry about the satellites any longer than was absolutely necessary.

As the second officer worked his helm controls, it occurred to him that he had done it. He had saved his landing party *and* prevented the aliens from wreaking havoc on Sordinia IV.

It gave him a distinct feeling of satisfaction. And maybe, in some small way, it made up for the tragic mistake he'd made back on the *Farragut*. At least, he wanted to think so.

As Kirk pondered that possibility, the turbolift doors opened behind him and someone came out. Glancing over his shoulder, he saw who it was—and couldn't help noticing the newcomer's expression. It was far from amiable, the second officer reflected.

"Kirk," growled Gaynor.

The security chief came down past the rail and approached the second officer, his mouth twisted with animosity, his face livid with barely contained emotion. And, though Kirk hadn't noticed it at first, the man still had a phaser planted in his fist.

The second officer got up from his seat.

"You were a whole lot luckier than you deserved to be," Gaynor snarled menacingly. "You should have pressed the damned trigger when I told you to. You should have—"

Before he could finish his sentence, Kirk drew his fist back and drove it hard into the man's face. Gaynor swayed for a moment. Then his knees gave way and he hit the deck—at which point the second officer grabbed his wrist and wrested the phaser pistol from him.

No one moved. No one said anything. They all just stared at the security chief as he lay crumpled on the floor. Then, little by little, Gaynor began to open his eyes. With an effort, he sat up and wiped a dark strand of blood from his mouth.

When he saw Kirk standing over him, an expression of disgust distorted his features. "Are you out of your mind?" he mumbled.

The second officer replied in a firm but even tone. "I should point out, Lieutenant, that I'm not the one who came storming onto this bridge with a phaser pistol in his hand. Nor, I might add, am I the one who decided to question the judgment of my commanding officer in public. Nor, finally, am I the one who defied that officer's orders by heading in this direction instead of sickbay."

The older man looked at him for a second, dumbfounded. Then his expression hardened again. "I'll have a few choice words about my commanding officer's judgment in my report," he said. "Make no mistake."

"That's your prerogative," Kirk told him. "After all, you were the officer in charge of the landing party. But you'll have to make that report from the brig." And with a gesture, he indicated that he wanted Masefield to escort Gaynor there immediately.

The security chief glowered at the second officer a moment longer. Then he turned and headed for the turbolift. Masefield followed. In a matter of seconds, both men were gone.

The second officer glanced at his friend, daring the navigator to say something. Gary returned the look for a moment, then turned his attention back to his control panel.

Sitting down, Kirk tapped his intercom stud again. "Kirk to sickbay. Dr. Velasquez . . . what's the situation down there?"

He heard the medical officer sigh. "Stable. How's the situation up there?" Velasquez asked.

"Stable," the second officer assured her. "I don't think we'll be sending any more personnel down there for a while."

"That's good," the doctor responded. "I've got all the company I care for right now."

"How's Medina?" Kirk asked. "And the landing party?"

Velasquez grunted. "Medina's fine. Chafin and Reboulet took a fair amount of punishment, but they'll be all right, too."

"I'm glad to hear it," the second officer told her. "Kirk—"

"Not so fast," the doctor interrupted. "First, I've got something to say to you, Lieutenant."

"What's that?" Kirk wondered.

"Congratulations," Velasquez said soberly. "It sounds like you did all right, all things considered."

"Thanks," he replied, trying not to blush. "Kirk out."

By then, the next satellite was in phaser range. The second officer checked to make sure its shields were down. Then he gave the order, and Masefield blasted it out of space.

Two down, thought Kirk, and four to go. . . .

Chapter Sixteen

SITTING DOWN in the *Constitution*'s center seat again, the second officer regarded the image of his captain on the forward viewscreen. Augenthaler was alone in the room. Apparently, he thought, Prime Vodanis and Commander Hirota were occupied elsewhere.

"The bombardments seem to have stopped for the moment," the captain noted. He frowned at Kirk. "I sincerely hope you're not going to tell me that's a temporary condition."

The second officer resisted a smile. "I don't believe the satellites will give you any more trouble, sir," he reported.

"Because . . . ?" Augenthaler prodded.

"Because we've destroyed them all," Kirk explained.

"Destroyed them?" the captain echoed, sounding a bit skeptical. "You mean all of them?"

"All except one, sir," said the second officer. "And that one has been disabled and taken aboard for study. After all, we never determined who the aliens were or why they came here."

Augenthaler's brow wrinkled. "Good point."

"Also," the younger man continued, "we destroyed an alien vessel."

"There was a vessel, too?" the captain asked, making no effort to conceal his surprise.

"There was, sir," Kirk confirmed. "Shortly after its arrival, it began coordinating the efforts of the satellites. There was no way to end the bombardment other than to obliterate it."

Augenthaler looked impressed. "Sounds to me like you did a masterly job up there, Lieutenant."

"That's kind of you, sir," Kirk responded, "but there are others who deserve credit as well. Lieutenant Mitchell, Ensign Wooten, Lieutenant Masefield, and Lieutenant Medina, for instance, for making critical contributions on the bridge. And then there are Lieutenant Gaynor, Lieutenant Borrik, Lieutenant Polcovich, and security officers Reboulet and Chafin, who transported aboard the enemy ship and disabled its link with the satellites."

The captain looked at him with even greater respect. "Transported aboard, you say?"

"Yes, sir," Kirk confirmed.

The older man harrumphed. "That must have been a tricky maneuver."

"It required a good deal of coordination," the

second officer admitted. "But we managed to pull it off."

"Apparently," said Augenthaler. "I'll want to hear more about it when I get back, of course."

"Of course, sir," Kirk replied. He felt his mouth go dry. "Unfortunately, I also have some fatalities to report."

The captain's features hardened perceptibly. "Go ahead," he said.

The second officer swallowed. "Lieutenant Lynch, Lieutenant Jankowski, and security officers Park and Zuleta gave their lives in the line of duty. They were killed when the alien vessel blew up one of its satellites."

Augenthaler's mouth twisted with grief as he considered the loss of his friends and colleagues. But he was a captain; he couldn't dwell on it. So he took a deep breath to steady himself, then let it out.

In the end, all he said was "Acknowledged, Lieutenant."

Kirk didn't know where Commander Hirota was at the moment, but he was certain the exec would be even more aggrieved—especially when he heard about Lieutenant Jankowski. He didn't envy Augenthaler the duty of having to tell Hirota what had happened.

Abruptly, a couple of Sordinians entered the picture from the background. The second officer didn't recognize either of them, but the captain clearly knew who they were. He turned away from the viewscreen to exchange a few clipped sentences with them.

When Augenthaler turned to face Kirk again, he

seemed more weary than saddened. Apparently, there was still a great deal for the captain to do on the planet's surface.

"It seems we've still got some work ahead of us," he told the second officer. "At least until we can assure the Sordinians that they're out of the woods. I'll contact you when we need a ride up."

"Aye, sir," said Kirk. "We'll be waiting."

The captain nodded. "Augenthaler out."

A moment later, the captain's image vanished from the viewscreen, giving way to the blue-green expanse of Sordinia IV. The second officer took a moment to scan the faces all around him.

Gary was still at navigation and Masefield was back at weapons control, but Wooten had been replaced at the communications station by the remarkably durable Lieutenant Borrik. Also, there was a crewman named Tomberlin at the helm and another named Herzog at the science station. They all went about their business matter-of-factly, as if they and all their crewmates hadn't been fighting for their lives less than half an hour earlier.

But then, Kirk thought, that was how it was supposed to be. A Starfleet officer was supposed to be able to put tough times behind him. He was supposed to have the ability to move on.

And that was what the lieutenant was going to do at that very moment. He was going to forget everything he had been through and move himself off the bridge, into his bed.

After all, his regular shift had ended hours ago and he was bone-tired. And as they had told him back at the Academy, a tired commander was sometimes worse than no commander at all.

Kirk turned to the Dedderac. "You've got the conn, Mr. Borrik. Wake me if anything important comes up."

The communications officer nodded his striped head agreeably. "Aye, sir. I will, sir."

Getting up from the captain's chair, Kirk made his way around it and headed for the turbolift, looking forward to a respite. Then he heard a familiar voice say, "Lieutenant?"

Turning around by the rail, the second officer saw his friend Gary looking at him. "What is it?" he asked the navigator.

"Permission to accompany you, sir," said the junior officer.

His tone gave no hint of why he might want to do that. But Kirk thought he had an inkling. He considered the request for a moment or two.

Then he nodded and said, "Permission granted."

Mitchell waited just long enough for Herzog to arrive at the navigation console. Then he surrendered his post and followed the second officer into the lift compartment.

Kirk tapped the turbolift's command mechanism with the heel of his hand. "Deck Six," he said out loud—for his companion's sake—as he entered the information. "Section four."

Mitchell waited until the doors hissed closed, sealing them off from prying eyes and ears. Then he turned to his friend.

But Kirk turned to him at the same time, his eyes fierce with determination. "I know exactly what you're going to say, dammit. I didn't make the tough decision."

"Listen," Mitchell began. "I—"

"No, you listen," the second officer told him, poking a finger at his chest. "This wasn't a test. It wasn't the *Kobayashi Maru* scenario back at the Academy. This was a real-life problem, with real-life consequences. And it was more important for me to keep my people alive than to prove myself to anyone—you included."

Mitchell shook his head. "You're so—"

"Besides," Kirk went on, "who made you the arbiter of right and wrong? You've never commanded anything in your life. How could you possibly know what it's like to sit in the captain's chair?"

"That's exactly—"

"I took what I decided was a calculated risk," the second officer declared. "And you know what? I got away with it, didn't I? I saved Gaynor and the others and I achieved our objective anyway."

"If you'd just—"

"To me," said Kirk, "that's reason for celebration, not insubordination and defamation and abuse from my navigator and my chief of security and who knows who else."

"Jim, I can't believe—"

The second officer pounded his fist into the palm of his other hand. "For crying out loud, Mitch, that's the way Garth of Izar operated. He didn't try to equate one experience with another. He identified each situation as a unique set of problems and opportunities, then acted accordingly. And from now on, that's the way Jim Kirk is going to operate as well."

Mitchell held his hands out. "Dammit, Jim, I'm not going to—"

"Don't argue with me," Kirk warned him. He turned away from his friend and pulled down on the front of his uniform. "Anyway, what's done is done. Period, end of story. If you're bound and determined to be disappointed in me, I guess there's not a whole lot I can do about that."

Suddenly, Kirk whirled and the navigator found himself nose to nose with him once more. The man's eyes had narrowed, and his finger was poking in the direction of Mitchell's chest again.

"But I'll tell you what," Kirk snapped. "If I had to do it all over again, if I were faced with the same situation a second time, I'd do it exactly the same way. No question about it."

Finally, it seemed, he had run out of ammunition. Mitchell looked at him. "Are you done?" he asked.

The second officer considered the question. "Yes," he responded at last. "I'm done, all right."

"You're sure?"

"Quite sure."

"Then let me say what I came here to say in the first place. What you did took courage . . ."

Kirk looked surprised.

". . . and instinct . . ."

He looked even more surprised.

". . . and a recklessness," Mitchell said, "that I've seen in only one other person—the individual I admire most in the entire world." He smiled. "In other words, me."

The second officer was clearly at a loss for words. His mouth gaped, but nothing came out.

"What's more," said Mitchell, "you did it while everyone including me was telling you to do otherwise. You stuck to your guns, pal. You persevered despite everything. And, as you so eloquently point out, you made exactly the right decision."

Kirk looked a little sheepish. "Uh . . . thanks," he replied.

The navigator pointed a finger at him. "But that doesn't mean you're off the hook," he said.

The second officer seemed confused. "It doesn't?"

"Not by a long shot. The day's still going to come when you've got to make the tough decision—when you've got no choice but to cut your losses, no matter who or what those losses might be."

His friend looked at him. He didn't say anything, but it was clear he was considering the comment.

"What if your window of opportunity had been half as big?" Mitchell asked. "A tenth as big? Would you have been able to sacrifice your people then? What if . . . what if it were your best friend on the line?"

Kirk frowned at the suggestion. "Tell you what," he said. "Let's hope we never have to find out."

The man was holding something back. Mitchell could tell. He had an impulse to press the issue, to find out what Kirk would do in such a situation . . . but in the end, he refrained.

After all, the navigator liked the bit of swagger the second officer had discovered in himself. He liked it enough, in fact, to overlook whatever shortcomings it might conceal. Besides, he had a feeling that he and Kirk would have this conversation again sometime.

Just then, the lift doors opened on Deck Six. Mitchell and his friend looked at each other for a moment. It appeared they had found a common ground—a place where they could both accept the things that had happened and move on.

The navigator shook his head. "You know, if you hadn't gone charging ahead with your assumptions instead of listening to me—"

Mitchell heard footsteps. Peering out of the lift, he saw a pair of crewmen coming down the corridor. He waited until they had passed by, then lowered his voice so he wouldn't be heard by anyone except Kirk.

"This conversation could've been a damned sight shorter," he said, finishing his sentence. He grumbled. "Back at the Academy, you said your middle name was 'Racquetball' . . . remember?"

Recalling the incident, a lopsided grin took over Kirk's features. "I did say that, didn't I?"

"Well," Mitchell told him, "from now on, it's 'Rhinoceros.' "

The other man shrugged, conceding the point. "If you say so."

Silence, for a moment. Not the uncomfortable kind, either.

"Anyway," the navigator said, "I'm glad things worked out."

Smiling tiredly, Kirk nodded. "So am I."

"See you later, then?"

"Later," the second officer agreed.

Mitchell watched Kirk exit the turbolift and head for his quarters, looking as tired as the navigator had ever seen him. If there was any justice in the world, he mused, his friend would lose consciousness as soon as he hit the sack and sleep the sleep of the guiltless.

Certainly, Kirk had earned it.

Chapter Seventeen

KIRK BLINKED, remembering where he was. On the *Enterprise,* not the *Constitution.* And he wasn't a second officer anymore. He was the captain of his own ship.

But all these years later, Kirk still remembered the look on Gary's face as he left the navigator there in the turbolift. At the time, it had appeared that Gary accepted his pal's explanation for the things he had done in the captain's chair. It had appeared that Gary understood his rationale for the life-and-death choices he had made.

Of course, Kirk hadn't told his friend the whole story. He could admit that now, if only to himself.

He had held back, because, at that point in his career—that point in his life—he still wasn't sure he could make the tough decisions. He wasn't certain, as the two of them stood there wearily in a lift compartment on the *Starship Constitution,* that he could have let one of his people perish under any circumstances.

The captain sat back in his chair and heaved a sigh. What would Gary think of him now? he wondered. What would he think of the way Kirk had handled the lastest threat to the *Enterprise?*

After all, he had seen the kind of threat into which Gary was evolving. He had watched it happen, hour by hour, and he had attempted to convince himself that everything would be all right. It was only after Spock had provoked him, even suggesting that he kill his friend in cold blood, that Kirk had ordered Kelso to chart a course for Delta Vega.

Gary himself had acknowledged the captain's wisdom in attempting to abandon him on the planetoid. *What would you do in my place?* Kirk had asked him at one point. And his friend had smiled an eerie smile.

Kill me, he had advised. *While you can.*

And even then, Kirk hadn't quite learned his lesson. He still hadn't been able to make the tough decision.

Shortly after Gary had broken free of his prison on Delta Vega, the captain had found himself holding a boulder high over his head, with a chance to destroy the monster his friend had become. But Kirk had hesitated for just a moment—and that hesitation had nearly proved his undoing.

Lightning-quick, Gary had seized the boulder and tossed it away. And then he had tossed the captain away as well, as if he were an insignificant piece of debris.

It was only when Kirk got his third chance to kill Gary that he had finally done what was needed. He had seized the opportunity as a drowning man seizes a piece of flotsam in a raging river.

Skidding down an incline, the captain had grabbed the phaser rifle his friend had knocked out of his hands. He had aimed it at the colossal rock hanging precariously over Gary's head, which Gary himself had carved out of the barren cliffside.

And he had fired.

Thinking about it, Kirk found himself adjusting his cast again. He would never forget the look on his friend's face—the realization that, despite all his power, he had somehow lost the battle. But maybe, just maybe, some surviving part of Gary had seen Jim Kirk make the toughest decision of his life and applaud him for it.

At long last, he had learned what his friend was trying to teach him that day so long ago. Before it was too late for him and the rest of the galaxy, he had made the tough decision.

The captain shook his head sadly. Back at the Academy, he had been Gary's instructor. His teacher. But at that moment, he wasn't sure who had learned more from whom.

As for the aliens, whose name turned out to be the N'shaii . . . with their takeover of Sordinia IV frustrated by the *Constitution,* they had to have seen they weren't invincible. They might have learned from the experience and steered clear of the Federation from that time onward.

But they didn't.

They crossed swords with Starfleet vessels on five subsequent occasions. First at Velarrh VII, where it was the *Excalibur* that sent them packing. Then at Mos'rammi IX and Indish III, where they fought the *Lexington* and the *Potemkin,* respectively. Then again at Linyar II, where they encountered the *Excalibur* a second time. And finally at Tenekratus IV, where they fell to the phasers of the *Defiant.*

After that, the N'shaii either gave up trying to seize other people's planets or took their aggression elsewhere. Starfleet Intelligence believed it was the latter, naturally.

Of course, the aliens might have prevailed if not for the sacrifice made by Lynch, Jankowski, and the two security officers who died along with them. Thanks to the data they downloaded to the *Constitution*'s computer, Federation scientists even figured out how to deal with the N'shaii's muon beams before too long.

But it wasn't until much later, after the invaders had been soundly thrashed, that Kirk's people learned about the N'shaii themselves. What they discovered was interesting, to say the least.

Originally, he and his colleagues on the *Constitution* had speculated that the aggressors wanted Sordinia IV for its natural resources. Nothing could have been further from the truth. In fact, the N'shaii had been playing a game of three-dimensional chess.

It came to light that there was not one group of N'shaii, but several—each one a political faction that had been competing with rival factions for thousands upon thousands of years—and one of their favorite forms of competition was to see who could conquer and hold the greatest number of populated planets. Needless to say, it was a sport appreciated more by the conqueror than the conquered.

Kirk gazed at the *Enterprise*'s viewscreen, where fields of stars streamed by at hundreds of times the speed of light. Too quickly, he told himself. Much too quickly.

With each passing moment, with each pinprick of a star the *Enterprise* overtook and left behind, they were getting closer to the planet Earth. Closer to the Mitchells and Gary's funeral service. Closer to the eulogy the captain had been asked to deliver.

How could he do it? he asked himself. How could he stand up in front of all Gary's friends and relatives and mourn the man's passing when it was he himself who had put an end to him?

Kirk readjusted his cast. He had made the tough choice, finally—the only choice he could have made under the circumstances. But his friend, his best friend, had perished as a result.

And when he got to Earth, the captain told himself, he would become the biggest hypocrite the galaxy had ever known.

Look for STAR TREK Fiction from Pocket Books

Star Trek®: The Original Series

Star Trek: The Next Generation®

Star Trek: Deep Space Nine®

Star Trek®: Voyager™

Flashback • Diane Carey
The Black Shore • Greg Cox
Mosaic • Jeri Taylor

#1 *Caretaker* • L. A. Graf
#2 *The Escape* • Dean W. Smith & Kristine K. Rusch
#3 *Ragnarok* • Nathan Archer
#4 *Violations* • Susan Wright
#5 *Incident at Arbuk* • John Gregory Betancourt
#6 *The Murdered Sun* • Christie Golden
#7 *Ghost of a Chance* • Mark A. Garland & Charles G. McGraw
#8 *Cybersong* • S. N. Lewitt
#9 *Invasion #4: The Final Fury* • Dafydd ab Hugh
#10 *Bless the Beasts* • Karen Haber
#11 *The Garden* • Melissa Scott
#12 *Chrysalis* • David Niall Wilson
#13 *The Black Shore* • Greg Cox
#14 *Marooned* • Christie Golden
#15 *Echoes* • Dean W. Smith & Kristine K. Rusch
#16 *Seven of Nine* • Christie Golden

Star Trek®: New Frontier

#1 *House of Cards* • Peter David
#2 *Into the Void* • Peter David
#3 *The Two-Front War* • Peter David
#4 *End Game* • Peter David
#5 *Martyr* • Peter David
#6 *Fire on High* • Peter David

Star Trek®: Day of Honor

Book One: *Ancient Blood* • Diane Carey
Book Two: *Armageddon Sky* • L. A. Graf
Book Three: *Her Klingon Soul* • Michael Jan Friedman
Book Four: *Treaty's Law* • Dean W. Smith & Kristine K. Rusch

Star Trek®: The Captain's Table

Star Trek®: The Dominion War

Star Trek®: My Brother's Keeper